I0716166

Sita Seecharrun Harris wrote her first short story at the age of fifteen, winning an award by Radio France Internationale. Born in Port Louis, Mauritius, she grew up in the capital, imbibing its tropical cosmopolitan vibe. She is a bilingual Writer, Designer, Illustrator, artist and Humanitarian Aid & International Development Expert. She lives with her husband in Longwell Green, Bristol, U.K.

From the same author:
When the Stars Shine
Taming of the Brew
The Curse of Bêti
Mystery of the Golden Idol of Khushipur (contributor)
The Lost World of Mû
Island Folk Stories of the Indian Ocean Vol1
Island Folk Stories of the Indian Ocean Vol2

The Lost World
of Mû

SITA SEECHARRUN HARRIS

To my mother who remains my inspiration.

To my husband who remains my anchor.

Table of Contents

Preface

I chose to write this novel because I have come to realise, quite lately, that I am, after all, a storyteller. That is probably due to my being an islander.

I don't come from just any island, but a special one. So tiny and so remote that the world's major colonial masters fought each other for its possession, for reasons only known to them. But the world hailed it due to the spice route wars to India.

Islands are perhaps where we are most likely to find littoral societies, for one would expect to find here a more concentrated mix of various cultural influences. Indeed, on smaller ones, there would be nothing but coastal people, for the sea would permeate the whole area. For many of my growing

years in the underbelly of the capital, with a small attractive port, I wondered why it was proven to be more efficient than the one built by the French, where they lost the island to the Brits. What chooses a good port? The wind, the tide, the depth at the shore ...? As a little girl, I didn't have many answers, but the horizon line fascinated me. I even swam many times to La Pointe, as Pointe aux Sables was known at the time.
My quest and attraction to the blue vastness never spilled over, nor did it quench my thirst for knowing more about 'our sea'. Inhaling the marine air differs each day, each month, and each season.

One has to be fused with it by the umbilical cord to understand the hues that a marine waft can carry, it's beyond the purity one can imagine.
It reminds me of Charles Trenet's 'La Mer'

and jolts in a calmness that touches the soul. I regarded this mesmerizing blueness as a fable long lost to the understanding of man. Humans are rather different here than other species.

'Beaches are beginnings and endings. They are the frontiers and boundaries of islands. For some life forms the division between land and sea is not abrupt but for human beings' beaches divide the world between here and there, us and them, good and bad, familiar and strange.'

The question is whether we can see people who live on the coast as making up a distinct society, one that can be separated from those further inlands. If so, can we find any commonality in littoral society all around the far-flung shores of the Indian Ocean?

Does location on the shore transcend differing influences from a very diverse inland, both in geographic and cultural terms, so that the shore folk have more in common with other shore folk thousands of kilometres away on some other shore of the ocean than they do with those in their immediate hinterland? Littoral society is usually considered to be the same as coastal society.

A sea-coast people, looking mainly to foreign lands and the ocean for livelihood and commerce, accustomed to seeing among them, not infrequently, men of dress, manners, and religion different from their own. Many of them themselves travellers or voyagers to Basra, Baghdad, Bahrain, Oman, and some even farther, are commonly free from that half-wondering, half-suspicious feeling which the sight of a stranger occasions in the isolated desert-girded centre. In short, experience, that best of masters, has gone far to unteach the lessons of ignorance, intolerance, and national aversion.

My island is not neat.

Not a single straight line on it. Not edged with tall white cliffs like meringue or skirted with little beaches padded flat as the edges of a pie. You couldn't compare it to any foodstuffs at all, and not sweet ones. Maybe, a pear, if that is to choose a fruit. Not the elegant William but a rather stout one at the belly, as if it had an equator which inflated its waistline. Its cliffs and clusters of defiant trees and rain-blown small sandy coves bunched around invisible fences, for here, there were no known boundaries except those laid by egotistical land barons and nouveau riches who erected second homes looking defiantly towards the sea as if to say 'look! I have arrived'

In most places, you will find a low row of cottages painted chalky island colours with a preference for peach, green Alouda, and pink like a gato coco bien rose.

Be it a small harbour, a fish landing station, or a peninsula, it's never too far to reach the mainland, for there's only one. For it also doesn't matter how hard it is to get there, or how tall the waves are when a cyclone blows over the island.

Everyone can reach anywhere. Things are notoriously kept behind a line of decency when it comes to the elements going wild.

Someone called it a paradise once and a writer even said that paradise was modelled upon it.

Anyone will happily tell you that while boasting about the beauty of the island but just try and touch how men behave among themselves and you will set hell in wrath.

People here are great gossip mongers. Islanders are good at that. Mix a cool beer or cheap white rum and you will untie tongues in seconds.

What other choice do we have?

Every childhood is an island.

For it is a sheltered place far from any land which can shine upon us. We are wrecked by our isolation.

In mercy and bliss.

I was born on this island.

I have intentionally included some French Patois Creole expressions and words coupled with French to give the narrative its authentic feel of the island of Mauritius.

"The more clearly we can focus our attention on the wonders and realities of the universe about us, the less taste we shall have for destruction."

Rachel Carson

"Myths which are believed in, tend to come true."

George Orwell

'A mighty empire once ruled the larger part of the world. Its rulers lived in a vast citadel, up against the sea, a great maze of corridors like nothing seen since. They were indigenous workers in gold and ivory and fearless bullfighters. But then, for defying Poseidon the Sea God, in one mighty deluge the citadel was swallowed beneath the waves, its people never to be seen again.'

1

Crab on the rocks

The high melodious notes of the morning call to prayer floated over us. That meant it was almost six a.m. The sky was still dark, but a lighter pinkish hue at the horizon promised dawn was almost with us. This was the only time the air was slightly chilly in Port Louis, and I shivered, enjoying the sensation. It lasted only a few weeks as for the rest of the year it was balmy and humid. Sparkling dewdrops highlighted beautiful cobweb patterns on the roadside lower branches of the mango tree and the smell of night jasmine was sweet in the air.

I breathed in the promise of a new day.

It felt good to be alive.

Better to be living with fools than dead in the company of sages, so they say.

It was early morning and the rain had stopped. The grass on the small lawn in the front of the timbered colonial house was still wet.

I remembered how yesterday unnerved me. Like a dream. It was years ago when something gripped the capital, choking it for answers. My return to my native city was fraught with growing years of decadence and modernity swaying at each other nonchalantly, in a way unique to island nations. Living in a vivid frenzy but drowned with equal veracity in limberness.

That night, I plunged into one of my recurring nightmares. The event of the day had precipitated one of my worst memories. And as we know such memories are a hard battle for the brain to bury.

There are heads floating all around, rising high on the waves before plunging down fast, roller-coaster against the wet shale sky. The water is bitter, and I'm pushed under again. I can't feel or move my limbs nor do I see them yet I'm moving so fast that my eyes, raw with burning salt, are unable to process the changing snapshots of sky and water. I catch a glimpse of Mother's face again; her eyes are ripe with fear. Somewhere in another great swell, I lost Mother's hand. 'Mother? Mother? Mother!'

I am that lost child in a crowd again, feeling her hand slip from mine. I'm falling. I hear screams and see the faces of my other traveling companions full of panic. They don't seem to see me. I lock with a pair of bewildered eyes for a moment. A woman's, sea-green and two perfect mirrors of the water. Her head turns before I can make out the face. Then the hands grab her. I'm thrown high again by another wave. The hands are on Green Eyes' shoulders, making their way spider-fast to the crown of her head. Her eyes are wide and pleading now. Fear and desperation reflect on their surface. Then the thin-boned hands push down on her delicate head and the green eyes disappear beneath a spume of white water. Her small hands reach up and twist with tiny dancer's fingers. Whoever reaches out and pushes the woman down again has their back to me. She struggles free for a moment, her mouth gasping above the water, her head tilted back against the waves. The mouth lingers open as if caught on a word that is instantly swept away. Her head is forced below once more. At that moment, it's as if I'm looking at them from the other side of a window. I see the final push below the waves. Those perfect stained-glass eyes linger on the surface of my thoughts before dissolving into the sea. She is gone. Another swathe of water covers me. I'm washed below the waves and carried. I struggle to the surface and scream out to stop.

There's no one there.

Green Eyes has gone, swallowed by the sea. What was in these angry waves? I look down. I must be crazy. I try to calm my reckless breaths. There were hands that pushed her down, I know there were. But whoever it was, has collapsed into nothing but foam. I can't find the light of the green eyes anymore either. They linger in my imagination, thick with a film of watery fear, pleading for help. I close my eyes so I can't see the body falling lifelessly towards the sea's deep floor. The falling sensation wakes me in a jolt.

My light sweat around the girdle of my neck, and racing heart rate tell me that I am alive and breathing .... awake! Thankfully.

This island keeps its secrets.

Of lives lost, of fates twisted, of deep sufferings, of painful longings. It took me many years before I could brace it and return to my island. I had tried all manner of therapies to heal, to forget and forge a new me. Suffice it to say that there needs to be just one tiny trigger and it all comes flooding back. That body washed up on the beach. It completed that task, now I will need to know how to navigate, to re - bury my memories.

I get up from the bed, walk towards one of the windows, open it to let the morning sun inundate me with its warmth. I try to remember my dream, it comes in flashes. Good enough to send a wariness, a feeling which is not very welcome on waking up. I thought I would be alive, kicking full of buzz. Tragedies can weigh the soul in ways no one can imagine.

People who live through a disaster somehow seem to attract even more tragedy, as if fate has found a new lightning rod. Calamity and chaos seem to gravitate towards certain individuals.

I shudder at the same time thinking of that body. Who could it be? It certainly has tasted death in the sea like many unknown ones. Will I die in the sea one day? Am I ill-fated by the family tragedy to finish like this? No, not yet. There is more to life to contend with. Death will have to wait. Death is always waiting. It comes rushing in a blink if one is not cautious.

Freshly brewed vanilla tea wafts into my nostrils. The help was here, and the first thing she did was make tea. A pot for me and a mug for her. There's something very heart-warming about smelling vanilla tea in Mauritius. It pulls at all the right strings of the heart to a world of familiarity. I drag my feet towards the welcoming aroma. Passing by each room brushed with the insinuation of past lives, remnants of their voices whispering through the walls.

A wood pigeon cooed rhythmically by the window bars, lulling the house into a composed, comfortable cocoon. This shambling, aged house did still breathe with a little life. There were distant echoes of joy here, but it felt morose now.

The tall mottled mirrors peered from shadows, eager to capture new faces. So many faces remembered in their silvered surfaces, each lingering on that lost moment when someone looked deep into the watery depths, a tiny fragment of them caught there forever.

For me, it was a new day, I am trying to recapture my lost thoughts. Make the house trust me again, believe in my presence. Swati greets me as I reach the kitchen. 'Bonjour Madame' she gently puts a pot of tea on the table, she gathers a mug, a small jug of hot milk, just as I like it and a small spoon, all set on a woven rattan tray. What an agreeable way to start the day.

*

Mornings are magical on islands, especially in Mauritius. I had walked across to the sand and then right up to the water's edge. Forgot to say, the house was sprawling on a wide battered garden with 'pieds dans l'eau' everyone's dream place on the island. But Baie du Tombeau is Baie du Tombeau. No point in comparing it to the ideal blazing tourist spot like Grand Baie. Here, it's the poor man's Côte d'Azur and no one complains about the lack of infrastructure or flashy hotels.

Children played in the red-coloured earth, unscathed by the lack of glamour in their surroundings. The only flashy sign of big concrete buildings was a dead Chinese smart city with humongous karaoke parlours and stages where promises were stronger than actual reality. It was a deal between China and Mauritius to revitalise the bilateral friendship and financial support the Oriental giant gave to the tiny island nation for its handful of Chinese immigrants. Besides it all, life went on among the locals.

Old fishermen hung out at the lone *boutik Sinwa* sipping their rums at any time of the day till their lips run discoloured and pink, in a true *laraker* (drunkard) style. The youth kicked football at dusk and jogged in the glorious early morning sunrise. Life in short was quiet and unassuming.

The beach was not private, but there was no one else there at that hour. The combination of dawn and low-tide debris gave the impression of old secrets washed up, ready to be revealed.

A light breeze came across the water, bringing the smell of salt and distant decay as well; this being Port Louis or neighbouring Roche Bois, Batterie Cassé to be precise. The industrial plants nearby, exuded their tuna and Agro chemical odours. Even if the light emerald sea before me showed distant tankers and cruisers, it was still a boundary and a reminder that somewhere beyond them there was a vital ocean and living planet.

Like many other city and office-bound people, the two were unfamiliar with the experience of being exposed to the wind, the waves, and physical space. Little did I know that after such a blissful moment, my life was going to change.

"Guétté, enn krab lor ross!"

I looked towards the voice and saw two young boys playing fishing with a condensed milk tin stripped of its label around which were wound yards of nylon thread. Each had a bamboo cane as a fishing rod, and I would guess a small artisanal bait hanging to catch some small fish. If they were lucky, a mackerel or two.

'There's something over there!' One of them said. I followed in the direction of his gaze, squinting over the beach.

'Where? I shouted in their direction.

They turned towards me and one pointed out to the shore.

"Over there. It looks like a jellyfish; is it? It's huge!"

It's not a jellyfish. It's just a plastic bag . . ."

"Yes, it's a jellyfish—I can see its body and its legs and everything. Can't you see? I think it's dead. Are there poisonous jellyfish around Baie du Tombeau?" One approached the floating 'jellyfish'. He seemed to smell it, before realising it was no jellyfish.

He screamed.

He ran back.

He stopped sharply and vomited.

Then, they put on their gritty sandals and ran back towards the road.

I called 'What is it?'

'*Ene dimoun mor sa*!". (It is a dead body)

I was stunned, unable to move.

2

Ah Cheew

'Now they are finding bodies on the beach! I tell you, that place is bad luck! *mo dire ou.*'

News that an unidentified woman's body had been found washed up on the beach at Baie du Tombeau, in a plastic bag, had not made it into any of the morning papers, but it had been the hottest news online and over the radio at the ten o'clock news.

The bible prayers, read after that couldn't be more fitting. Some peace was required for that poor departed soul.

Ah, Cheew held a small café shop in

Chinatown, less than a minute's walk from Queen's Street. It was well-known for good traditional Chinese food and famous for the no-nonsense dishes Ah Cheew had been selling out of her house for years.

Ah Cheew's Delights was also equipped with the latest modern equipment. Gone are the days, when her forefathers came to the island and settled in the capital, limited to manual trades they could carry on. They relied on their abacus to count the money coming in while breaking their backs for ironing, making handmade noodles and dumplings, funeral paper offerings and traditional Chinese sweets.

Though she was revered for cooking to the traditional standards, strange dishes occasionally popped up because Ah Cheew loved experimenting. In her view, anything cooked with local ingredients was local food. The shop was very like Ah Chew herself.

Another passion of hers was reverse engineering dishes (and occasionally people) to figure out how they had come about and how they might be better adjusted. Her *boulettes* and Saw Mai carried an umami flavour which many housewives have tried demystifying to no avail. She always trusted her farmer cum vegetable seller from Crève Cœur, Manoj who fills her with fresh herbs and plump Kiew choy and choy sum greens, and his garlic chives are always extremely fragrant. Alongside the fresh chicken and eggs, she gets from Ton Lam, Ah Cheew made sure her dishes were concocted with the best ingredients.

All day Ah Cheew had been following news reports on radio and television and had even sent Nina round to the street corner to pick up the afternoon papers, but she hadn't learned any more about the body that had been found. She and Nina had overdosed on

DJ chatter and music (which Nina had quite enjoyed when Ah Cheew was not changing channels, hoping for more news), but all she had gotten were news updates without new information. She only received speculation from half-drunk customers. Was it the body of a gambler from the casino at Royal Street? Illegal immigrants, these days Bangladeshis are everywhere, who is it? Someone who has had a pay cut or an ill-fated love affair? Or an unlucky sailor? Had it been an accident, a suicide, or—most exciting of all—murder? It's not some kind of news this sleepy part of the capital was used to.

"Did you taste the sauce yet?" Nina reminded her boss. Though Nina did most of the food preparation now, Ah Cheew still calibrated the final seasonings. She moved across to taste the sweet and tangy chili sauce again. It was in the sauces and seasonings, as she constantly reminded

Nina, that the real art of cooking was to be found. And it was no use asking for exact measurements either. There were no exact measurements; it was more a matter of training your taste to recognize the perfect pitch so that you could always rely on yourself to adjust the ingredients to hit precisely the right note. What good were recipes that gave you pounds and ounces—or worse, grams and litres—when how much a dish required depended on the quality and age of your ingredients?

Nina watched as Ah Cheew added a dash of coriander and a spoonful of tamarind pulp before giving the sauce a good stir. Nina keeps on trying at home in the hope that one day she can surpass her boss and win herself an acknowledgment with a bonus. A pay raise is all a distant dream, as Ah Cheew controlled every penny and was a Queen of thriftiness.

'I'm going to keep the TV on during tonight's dinner,' Ah Cheew said. 'Doesn't matter what the show is. Sometimes they have those breaking news announcements.' The murder mystery had certainly made a dent in the routine thinking of the middle-aged lady.

'Besides, if we don't pay attention to what's happening, who is going to?' Ah Cheew thought that the killer must be on the prowl, and who knows he might even have come to the shop today? Anything is possible. She switched on the radio and waited. The peppy voice of the newsreader announced the breaking news!

'Even if it wasn't a murder case, it's so gruesome to think of all those people enjoying themselves in the holiday resort while someone is lying dead on the beach, don't you think? Maybe it's a publicity stunt by the resort. Next, they'll announce there's a murder mystery competition—dead body washed up on Baie du Tombeau, did the ghosts of murdered dolphins do it?'

'*Ayoo! A la Wakashio ré vini* encore' sighed Ah Cheew pulling out a colander of bean sprouts to sort, making time for a chore while listening to idle radio blabber. Nina came closer with a frown, and checking on her boss's attitude asked, 'But Madame do dolphins have ghosts too?'

Ah Cheew looked at her and shook her head. 'Nina my girl, do I have to tell you that too? Anything which dies becomes a ghost.' This was Ah Cheew's Chinese beliefs talking. Nina opened her mouth to utter something, but retracted.

For all good reasons. She was perplexed. Does it mean that all the cockroaches she has killed behind the shop's yard have become floating ghosts too? Phew! She never thought of that. Nina came hurrying now as Ah Cheew started to stand up.

"What do you want to get from the kitchen, madame? I will get it for you." Ah Cheew knew Nina was angry because she was calling her 'Madame' and making her obey the doctor's orders to rest her foot. She had developed painful varicose veins out of years of long hours standing to cook. Her gait also expanded considerably which added weight to her poor knees. When she passed by Nina, a whiff of Chinese ointment trailed after her.

"I want to get a ladder. So next time I can get things for myself without everybody making such a fuss."

"Next time you can tell me what you want, and I will get it for you. You don't need to climb around like a monkey!" Nina put a little basket of prawn crackers on Ah Cheew's table.

"Madame," she added before walking away.

The light fragrant crackers were crispy and

savoury but did not make Ah Cheew feel better.

At first glance Ah Cheew was a typical Mauritian Hakka Chinese woman. She was fair-skinned with plump high cheekbones enough to please the most demanding in-laws, and short enough not to embarrass the most average-height Chinese man, and the traditional kabaï- kabaya she wore sported austerity of hard days, but her rose-cut diamonds, set in handcrafted twenty-karat gold, were enough to impress the most snobbish of customers. She was enough of a busybody to stick her nose shamelessly into everyone's business, tenacious enough to follow through, and a *vié ross* "not scared to die" as she charged recklessly in search of answers—something which had led to her solving several family mysteries.

The recent murder that happened in Baie du Tombeau has piqued her curiosity. The identity of the body and the motive for the murder were two enigmas her middle-aged head was hell-bent on solving. But for now, counting the money was key.

Ah Cheew liked buffets. The curious, contented crowd of people roused memories of family feasts and celebrations, and the sheer abundance of food woke a purely animal joy that no written menu could equal.

Three big pots, the Mauritian traditional *dektis* containing homemade *rougay* - spicy tomato sauces - held high pride. As they ran down, Nina or one of her helpers added peanuts - her secret ingredient, chopped onions, chili peppers, and onion chives to fried sausages. As any Mauritian cook knew, it was the quality of your *rougay* that determined your cooking skills in the kitchen. Ah Cheew was very proud of hers.

Having no one to pass them on to was one of the few things that made her regret having no daughters of her own. Nina somehow was kind of a daughter to her, but the latter had a mind of her own.

'*Ene Porter are ou Madame!*' Shouted a stout man with shiny dark skin. Probably a stevedore from the port. There were queues of them on Fridays when they got their weekly pay. Lager beers and Guinness were the most popular buys. They ate fried '*corne*' fish with '*pima carri*' to wash away the bitterness of their drinks. Nina darted busier than most days and the hum at the back of the room seemed like there was a rooster fight going on.

Sometimes an insult flew but one Ah Cheew embraced cheerfully.

After all, knowing everybody's business was necessary if she wanted to feed everybody good cheap food, and surely there was nothing wrong with that.

This surprised Ah Cheew that more people did not feel that way. She kept her ears peeled on the bits of conversations for any hints of the news about the murder.

"This woman and her husband adopted a dog, a puppy, from us when we were running the RSPCA organization. It doesn't exist anymore, but she's suing the three of us because we were the ones she dealt with."

Ah Cheew looked puzzled. "She didn't like the dog?"

'Who didn't like what dog?' Replied Nina.

"She agreed to return it to us if she couldn't keep it. But instead, she had it put down and then lied that she had given it to a friend."

"I remember her now! The puppy killer!"

Ah Cheew thumped her stick against her chair in delight at remembering the case.

"The puppy killer! It was in the newspapers!" It has also been all over social media and even international newspapers. After all, nothing unites Mauritians like getting angry at something or someone, especially when they can feel self-righteously patriotic about it. Most times for petty matters, while making it a national debate of cursing the government.

These days the favourite buzzword is '*chatwa*' meaning boot licker in Hindi and Bhojpuri. Many have been glorifying the word with many expletives. The population is divided between those who are *chatwa*s and those who are not, the latter category having no specific word coined for them, as yet.

Ah Cheew glowed with satisfaction. "I thought the puppy killer and her family had left the island."

"They did," Nina snapped, "swearing never to return. But she's back."

Tega gulped the last drops of beer from the dark amber Stella bottle. Usually, this is enough to get him into his mood of telling stories, yet no one understood from where he fetched them. He always swore that his *Ammay* told him those tales since he was a little boy.

'Today, I will tell you where this body comes from, which was washed on the beach of Baie du Tombeau.'

Ah Cheew heard him loud and clear and stopped short. She turned towards him and picked up her stick wobbling her way toward the small gathering around Tega.

'So, you know where it comes from? Who was it?'

Tega lifted his hand in a gesture to hold on. He cleared his throat and started.

'Once upon a time, a solid landmass covered most of the Indian Ocean. Some call the vanished continent Lemuria. Some call it

Mû.' Now Tega was a clever boy who read a lot. He was jobless for a long time and joined the stevedores when his grandmother fell ill. He was an orphan and was brought up by his *Ammay.*

Someone shouted in the crowd 'Mû, is it not how Mauritius is called on the net?'

Tega waved to him and acquiesced with a smile.

'Whatever name you would like to use, Lemuria or Mû existed before recorded history and its beginnings occurred before the more famously known ancient civilization of Atlantis.

Not a trace of Lemuria or Mû can be found today but whispers of its possibility remain through legends and myths as well as references in paranormal sources. Some believe that all that has survived of this sunken continent are its lofty mountain tops known today as the Mascarene Islands.

Although plausible, this theory cannot be proven scientifically. It can only be believed or at least considered a probability.

Kumari Kandam is a mythical continent, believed to be lost with an ancient Tamil civilization, supposedly located south of present-day India in the Indian Ocean. Alternative names and spellings include Kumarikkandam and Kumari Nadu.'

Someone again shouted something at Tega.

'Tega of course your stories revolve only around you Tamils, who else?'

Tega shouted back *'Camwad* ... listen to what I am telling, then you can make up your own judgment.'

'Ok Frer'!

Tega resumed his story. Ah Cheew squinted her eyes to concentrate better and slurped the words of the half-drunk Tega. This time, he was saying something that was of interest.

'Shhhh ... everyone, listen to what Tega is telling you!' Ah Cheew stomped with force. Suddenly, like in a classroom, the shop went quiet. So, Tega continued: 'In the 19th century, some European and American scholars speculated about the existence of a submerged continent called Lemuria. According to some writers, an ancient Tamil civilization existed on Lemuria, before it was lost to the sea in a catastrophe.'

'*An sa mem ki dire Atlantide!*'

Tega turned to the tall lanky guy and calmly said 'I am talking of Mu and Lemuria, did I mention Antlantide or Atlantis? *Pas mêlanz Kalchool bêta...écouter avant.*'

The guy bent his head, losing face to have been torn down so politely.

Tega went on: 'In the 20th century, Tamil writers started using the name Kumari Kandam to describe this submerged continent. Although the Lemuria theory was later rendered obsolete by the continental drift theory, the concept remained popular among Tamil revivalists. According to them, Kumari Kandam was the place where the first two Tamil literary academies (sangams) were organized during the Pandyan reign. They claimed Kumari Kandam as the cradle of civilization to prove the antiquity of the Tamil language and culture.'

'*Ayo Bon dié la Tega kouma dire bisin ale lekol pou conpran ki to pe dire*' someone said in an exasperated tone.

'Shushhh... zot ô! Anyone who doesn't want to listen can pay and leave.' Uttered a visibly irritated Ah Chew from these interruptions.

'Merci Ah Cheew!' Bowed a thankful Tega.

'So, what was I saying? Yes, Kumari Kandam was located in the present Indian Ocean. Research says Kumari Kandam was connected with Madagascar from Africa and Australia. According to the research, the

Kumari Kandam was separated into two parts of land masses. The lower part was called Lemuria. Lemuria was closer to Antarctica.'

'Tega, were all the Lemurians like you, like a Tamil?' Asked Ah Cheew.

'I don't know, but surely what I read says that Lemurians were just like you and me. If you can imagine the differences in daily life between, say, the people of North America and Europe or Asia, then that will give you an idea of the sophistication these two societies achieved over some millions of years. We have not yet caught up with their advancements in energy and medical treatments. Later, you'll read that the few Atlantean survivors (and those who migrated before the final destruction) travelled in all directions, including Egypt, Guatemala, and the Yucatán, where they integrated with the much less developed populations. Can you imagine the displacement and rise of sea levels (and accompanying tsunamis) engulfing all the coastal towns around the world, wiping out any trace of their existence when the two continents sank? The largest religions of the world relate the story of a flood such as Noah and his ark. Archaeologists keep identifying civilizations older than the last one discovered, so we cannot dismiss all legends as old wives' tales. Let's begin our exploration in ancient times — before Adam and Eve, with the existence of these two continents and how they became inhabited 60,000 years before they destroyed themselves.'

<u>A bit about the background</u>

'The name Lemuria was given by geologist Philip Sclater in 1864. The other part was called Kumari. Kumari kandam was also connected with the Indian subcontinent.

Kumari kandam was the place where the first homo sapiens (present day humans) evolved and became civilized.

The civilization at Kumari kandam was once far more advanced than the rest of the world at that time. Many people and scientists around the world didn't agree with this theory except for a few people, as there was limited documentation to prove this theory.

It is being claimed that Kumari Kandam was ruled by the female rulers known as Kumari. Women of that land had the right to choose their husbands and the right to hold property while holding the highest status of the priesthood. It is said that Kumari Kandam belongs to the Goddess 'Kanyakumari'. And the Kanyakumari temple at the furthest southern tip of south India was established by the people who survived the flood which engulfed the whole continent.

Science explains elaborately the origin of the earth through the 'Big Bang' theory followed by the theory of Evolution that proves, systematically, the origin of living organisms including humans and their development which had taken millions of years to evolve and sustain. It is apparent that the land 'Gondwana' at the southernmost part of the earth gave way to the Kumari continent due to geographical changes. 'Gondwana' was a huge landmass and its separation was what the Tamil people called as 'Kumari Kandam' One part of Gondwana is what was grasped as Kumari Kandam which had been comprehended thousands of years before. Kumari Continent, which was at the Tropic of Cancer, was the ideal geographical environment for the origin of life. The remains of the inundated 'Kumari

Continent' are the present geographical maps universally accepted by geographers, historians, and archaeologists. Some research scholars are sceptical about the existence of the Kumari Continent. The prehistoric occurrences of the Kumari Continent are being found in the Thamizh literary works directly and in the bordering regions' literature, indirectly. Geographers also acknowledge the fact that the residual regions of the submerged Kumari Continent are part of the current geographical land mass that existed before the drift of continents. The obliteration of the Kumari Continent is stumbled on in many religious literatures of the world.

The deep-sea archaeological research at Poompuhar regions of Thamizh Nadu, today's Tamil Nadu, has furnished adequate amounts and more evidence of the sunken Continent.'

Tega was dry at the mouth, he had spoken for a long time. Little by little his audience thinned out, some were dozing with their heads bent on their chest, chock full of rum. Ah Cheew didn't stop listening though, in fact, she avidly drank Tegan's words.

When the latter stopped, she came out of her torpor. Others around him were surely navigating on a different plane, thanks to the alcohol.

'Tega, can you tell us more about the murder? This kumari thingy has dragged on for far too long, come to the point!'

Tega looked at Ah Cheew as if it was the first time, he saw her.

'Who are you?'

'Who am I? You sod ...you better go home now before your *Ammay* whacks you with a broom!'

Tega regained his mind and came back to reality.

'Ah Cheew, I couldn't see your face well in this obscurity, sorry'

'You better be, now what?'

Tega made a move to get up and lost a bit of his balance but steadied quickly. He took his shabby bag and walked to the entrance.

'Bye Ah Cheew, see you tomorrow!'

'Look at him! He leaves me high and dry in the middle of a long story ... *Tantion* Tega! I shall see that you don't get your beer tomorrow. Nina! Did you hear?'

Ah Cheew was visibly miffed and waddled back to her seat behind the counter. She started fanning herself hard as if the heat had twin-folded itself. Hers was a Chinese paper fan with a whimsical dragon print on it. No huff and puff to cool down from the dragon.

3

Beach house

I'll never forget the day I saw the villa for the first time, sparkling like a clean sheet in the sleepy Mauritian sun.

The shutters were the colour of pale lichen, and bright fuchsia and white bougainvillea trailed over the black lava rocks. It was a simple place, in a sparse colonial building, that was centuries old, as old as this oft-forgotten slip of an island itself. The house, dominated by views of the sea didn't hide a paint swirl of turquoise that met the darkest navy across the horizon, vast and unknowable and full of promise. The air seemed somehow to whisper with it, and I had this feeling, there in the warm, fruit-flavoured sunshine, the scent coming from the mango and papaya trees that had grown wild and abandoned in the forgotten garden, of something inside me, stirring. The feeling was powerful, yet fleeting, over in the length of a sigh, but for the first time in months, I felt something shift and, for a moment, as if just maybe, I would be all right.

The villa was a chapter from a familial past, long before my birth. It belonged to a sepia-coloured photograph of an almost-forgotten corner of my family history. People whose names had all but washed away by the changing tides. Yet, here I was.

Like a message in a bottle, washed ashore from the wide arms of the ocean, a long-ignored treasure.

After that strange find of the boys on the beach, I felt that somewhere someone's life had been destroyed. It felt strange. I almost ran my tongue over my lips to wipe away the saltiness of the sea air, as if it carried the dead body's taste with it. I peeped through the front window which gave a glimpse of the road.

Some men had gathered around the boys who were busy explaining. I thought for a moment then headed towards the phone.

Yes, I needed to inform the police of the macabre find. Someone had to do it.

Anyway, the police soon came asking questions, as my house was the property that had direct access to the beach. I had never intended to come back here. I thought nothing on earth would ever drag me back to this godforsaken place. I had returned from the other end of the earth, Brittany, a promontory of coast of bare rock and raging waves, wild and angry at the rest of the world, stubborn to the last.

But here, in this shaded calm tropical Baie du Tombeau, things were different.

The wind tore at my hair and I tasted the salt carried on it like old tears, with nothing to stop it.

Back in Lannion, in Brittany, the cliffs fell away beneath my feet and the sky. Most times, I forgot about the sky there. It just seemed so much bigger than anywhere else, a vast dome of shifting greys and a myriad of intense blues which could change like a transient mood. Sea and sky, and the rocks between, the white of foam and clouds, all the colours of the Atlantic. Bright overhead, darkening as it swept towards the far western horizon, where it deepened to indigo and blended with the endless sea. The glare here, is what spells it's a different world. It's full of light, as if the sun has shifted its working place to be here all the time.

The drama that unfurled in front of the beach house comes back every time I try doing something to focus my mind. But it sends a chill down my spine. After reading what has been said about that body, it was hard to believe that such a horrible crime could have been committed in this peaceful looking vista.

Well, hell hides behind heaven so they say.

I walked to the open veranda with a fresh grenadine juice and let the wind whisk my tears away. They rolled out of my dehydrated eyes with so much saline air. I fix my gaze on the distant place where the sea and the sky melt together, seamless and blue, threatening oblivion.

Around this side of the bay, the rocks are a curious mixture of colours: black, slate grey, white, yellow. All with the tell-tale tiny vesicles of their volcanic basaltic origins. The sand is the finest I have ever encountered.

Sometimes, a flying fish jumps out of water, probably trying to catch a glimpse of what the human world looks like. One of those adventurous ones.

Baie du Tombeau, somehow with its idyllic beauty, hides a darker secret. It was a popular hideout for pirates. Stories abound of fathers, grandfathers, great-grandfathers aplenty... fishermen, soldiers, swimmers and sailors.

Many taken by the sea.

She is a constant mesmerizer, drawing and claiming lives she believes belong to her. Islanders are like moths to the flame.

4

Valériane

Nina Joosery was the opposite of Ah Cheew in many ways.

Ah Cheew was a fair, plump, busybody, while Nina was thin, dark, and wished everyone would mind their own business as she preferred to keep herself to herself. She was not, however, as skinny as she had been when she first came to work for Ah Cheew and her late husband, years ago. Her working relationship with Ah Cheew wasn't bumpy. Her boss was as generous with food as with her advice. Nina was no longer the scared, inept young woman who had arrived hopeless at almost anything as simple as separating egg yolks from whites. Now she is a competent cook in the kitchen, skilled at the computer, and most importantly - financially stable. But one thing she wasn't keen on was her boss lady's incredible nosiness.

People may say that in Mauritius this is an inevitable characteristic of Chinese women. Only those in the know and probably those who lived in the capital would agree with that, but for now, Ah Cheew was as sticky and clingy as mussels on a rock.

The Chinese shop *la boutik sinwa* is often a live repository of gossip. Need an update? Go to the *boutik sinwa*, you get fresh news with as many details as you wish. Ah Cheew fed on this trait and had Nina by her side to unload all of it throughout the day.

The latter listened with one ear most of the time. However, when it came to her own life, Ah Cheew was far too intrusive. She had been trying to match make for her, and that with the Inspector of Police, Sanjiv.

The guy was a regular at the shop and had shown some sweet smiles towards Nina. To his usual stern face, this was like '*la lune Eid*' someone had said. Ah Cheew had not missed this detail and had since been very generous with the Inspector.

He worked in the neighbourhood's police station and was well respected.

'I think the Inspector likes you, you should be kind to him, who knows he could become your husband'

'What?! No, I don't need a husband,' snapped Nina.

Ah Cheew was still somewhat in awe of the Inspector. She had been on her way to tell him what cute and clever children he and

Nina could have together. And how true love would be enough to overcome any differences between her Muslim and his Hindu background. Her quick mind was also ticking for some inside information about crimes in the area, including the recent body retrieved at Baie du Tombeau.

Ah Cheew beamingly turned to Nina.

'Inspector Sanjiv likes potato and lamb curry, right? We can use these potatoes to make something nice for the people at the station. If they like them, maybe they'll even offer to pay and order more next time! How many people are at his office today? Do you know?'

'I don't know. I never talk to Inspector Sanjiv.'

Nina kept her eyes and hands focused on scraping thin strips down the length of a cucumber. Her expression hardened, and she was hell-bent on not giving in to Ah

Cheew.

'If I go away for one week, she will see she cannot do without me', thought Nina, then she will have to stop trying to get me married off.

In any case, Nina could not see herself being called Mrs Callychurn, as Sanjiv's wife. She shuddered at the thought and carried on peeling tiny garlic cloves.

*

The surroundings were dark, cold, and indicated impending rain. Near the bay, a woman stood still with her back towards the water, staring at the shore and the woods beyond.

Professor Valériane Ducasse felt the cool mist settling on her clothes and skin. She tried to control her shivering, as it was too dark to see her surroundings clearly. She didn't have any food with her, and she regretted not eating earlier. She was afraid that if she moved too much or shivered, she would be seen before she could see anyone. She knew that they would have smelled the food if she had any with her. She stood on the doorstep, waiting for something to happen.

Now that she knows they exist.

Now that they had been seen.

Now is the right time to ascertain that her life's work had not been in vain.

She heard footsteps and turned, squinting hard, but the moon had failed her. It wasn't them; she was sure of that. She doubted she would have been able to hear them. She really couldn't see who it was until the shape loomed up and stopped within touching distance.

"So, you came," she whispered to the figure. "I must admit, I'm surprised. Still, I am glad. A witness is essential. Keep your voice down." The other, who had started to say something, decided to say nothing.

"You came to be my witness, be quiet." Obeying orders, the other spoke in an almost inaudible whisper.

"What are we going to do?" "Do we wait?"

"Yes, patience ..."

Minutes passed, seeming like hours, but Professor Ducasse refused to light the dial of her field watch. It could spoil everything at a crucial moment. The night would be long. How long had it been already? She had to force herself to stay awake, no matter what, to remember her determination that this time would be the time.

This time she would have actual contact, no matter how tenuous, and even better, tonight she had a witness. All the years, all the ridicule, it all came down to this one night the time for her triumph was finally here. She could feel it.

"What are you doing?" Valériane asked,

irritated with the sudden restlessness of her companion.

"You're making too much noise. What do you want with a rock in your hand anyway?" It was too late. She took the first blow full in the face. It broke her nose and she gasped in astonishment, aspirating her warm blood. There wasn't even time for her to start choking before there was a second blow, knocking her flat on her back.

Now, she was helpless. The third blow crushed her face completely and smashed the back of her head against the flat top of the boulder upon which she lay.

She became completely still. Then, with an arcing swing, Valériane's witness slung the murder weapon far out into the bay. Slapping gloved hands together to rid them of grit from the stone, the witness no longer tried to be quiet.

In fact, in a loud voice that would have

driven away any shy creature said, "You can come out now if you want to. I'm leaving, and the Professor isn't going to bother you anymore."

Dead leaves rustled and pebbles crunched as the murderer walked away, and brought a plastic bag, dragged the body, tied it, and rolled it over his boat. He took it to the reefs and threw the heavy bag overboard hoping it would sink.

But days later, the sea rolled it back at the edge of the bay, as if to say, 'Humans sort out your crime yourselves'.

*

Two policemen in uniform, a detective in civil clothes, and the local police coroner came out of the police jeep.

A small crowd of curious onlookers had gathered around the boys who found the body. The police party who didn't like telling them to clear off, because normally they were all friends together. And they were prime to gather nuggets of first-hand information. Inspector Sanjiv was the first to speak.

"Nobody's going to the beach yet. Where did you put what you found?" asked Inspector Sanjiv.

Clive, a local fisherman, a tall, middle-aged, weather-beaten man, tough and wiry, with a calm face and little to say for himself, eventually spoke.

"There was nowhere else to put it. We laid a sack over the front of the beach ... there!'

Eyes followed his finger pointing to the misshapen sac with its macabre content and a row of anxious faces followed every movement and word of those who started to investigate.

A lame reporter from a local paper joined them. "It was this way... Let's begin at the beginning..."

Inspector Sanjiv was quick and made a sign for him to steer away from the spot. The place was cordoned off and soon another vehicle arrived, with even more police officers.

The amassed crowd seemed to disperse a bit but re-formed as the police officers got to their tasks. For now, nobody had been singled out. Inspector Sanjiv came to face the crowd. He waved his hand and disappeared only to reappear on the side of the street, starting a cigarette while waiting.

Sunset was soon falling, and on-shore lights were springing up in the tavern nearby and houses on the sea-front. The streetlamps of the town came on, infrequent naked bulbs with reflectors which cast yellow pools below and the growing darkness outside their orbits. The lights on the villas on the beach shone out and threw long reflections like silver paths across the water. The police crew left the spot with an ambulance carrying the body.

At the mortuary, the coroner got to work very promptly. The body was that of a fairly tall woman of early middle-age. Medical evidence showed that it had been in the water for a couple of days ... It had apparently been cladded in a shirt, cotton trousers and sandals. There were no signs of identification on the clothes, which bore certain proprietary labels of such general use as to be valueless. There was a fracture of the cranium of considerable size, too large to be caused by accident and probably made by a blunt instrument or rock. The face wasn't recognizable. The contents of the skull had almost completely disappeared, but the clothing had partially protected some of the organs and medical experts are of the opinion that the body was already dead when placed in the sea.

"Better tone it down a bit. Still too horrific," said the editor to the reporter who had tagged along and remained stuck as a barnacle. So, the official edition omitted all references to what the fish had eaten before the body was recovered.

When Ah Cheew read the newspaper the next morning, she gasped with horror. She read it twice, then thrice. Wobbled her way to Nina, busy at the chopping board with garlic chives which filled the room with pungency.

'Ayo Mama! Did you see what they discovered?'

'What?! Do you think I have had time to read the newspaper Madame?' That tone again. Ah Cheew grimaced and ignored her. She went on, 'they crushed the face and broke the skull! Who could have done such an evil act, bloody monster!'

Nina stopped and looked at Ah Cheew, in horror. Ah Cheew continued reading the article aloud to her. Her shock was too big, and she needed to vent her sentiment aloud. Nina was the best receptacle.

Outside, the *makatia* (sweet coconut bun) seller hailed '*makatia so so makatia soooo!*'.

Regulars waited for the old Muslim man with his white prayer cap and a flaming orange henna tinted beard. He was seen daily at the same time in the area, perched sideways on his bike. People in Port Louis reckon his *makatia* are the best on the whole island. Nina usually rushes to get a couple of hot *makatia* to accompany her favourite afternoon tea, of her favourite Trois Dames brand. She likes the *makatia* cut in half and lathered with butter, the mixture of melted butter with sweet coconut stuffing was just right to make her heave a sigh of relief when she could sit down for a tea break.

But today, her head was full of what Ah Cheew had just blurted out. It had cut her appetite with shock and disgust.

'Nina, are you there? You seem to have seen a ghost!'

'How well can I be after what you just have been reading to me?'

'Here we go ... I was only doing my civic duty. I need to let people around me know that there is a murderer on the prowl. What if you are attacked? Then you will blame me for not having told you!'

Nina shuddered at the idea of someone lurking around the corner of a street and bloodying her face. She will need some distraction to get this new fear out of her mind.

Ah Cheew can never hold her tongue. This leech of a woman, she is getting worse with age.

5

Shrava

While the storm raged outside, the skies turned black and the sea rose, lashing itself against the rock walls, they lost themselves in each other. And afterward... afterward, his smile faded like the first flower in the garden. Around her neck, she wore a golden star wrapped around a key and while she dozed, sated, and happy at last, he took it.

She woke up with a start and cried out in alarm.

'Give it back.'

'Alas, that I cannot do,' he replied, mocking her.

The kindly, courtly lover was gone. He made for the door without a backward glance.

'Then die, faithless traitor!'

She spat the words at him, summoning powers that commanded the wind and the wave, magic taught to her by Shri Mani himself, the guardian of priests. Alas, nothing happened.

'Your magic has no power over me, princess,' said her latest lover disdainfully. Remember I am protected by the mighty gods themselves. A gift from you.'

The princess wrapped in a stole and rushed after him. Though she ran and he walked, she couldn't catch him. Invisible weights dragged at her as if she were running through deep water. Nor could she seem to raise the alarm. Her voice didn't carry any sound.

Her lover strode onwards, and she followed him out to the sea wall, to the great gates, which strained under the press of the wild waves. From across the courtyard, he smiled back at her, triumphant, as he slid the key into the lock on the sea gate and opened it to the raging ocean.

'Are you mad?' she screamed over the roar of the storm.

'You'll kill us all. The city will drown.'

'Oh yes,' he replied.

'The sea will have you. This is my intent.'

'But why?' 'Why? For every death, for every life exploited, for every family destroyed by you and your kind. I am the priestess of my people, their protector. And … you love me.'

'Love you?' A loud evil laugh concluded the answer.

The water was rising now, and he stood above it on the wall leading back to the precipice, to safety. It rushed towards her.

She saw her people begin to panic and flee, saw her father on his magical horse, riding across the waves, and for a moment she thought he would rescue her. But the elder priest behind him damned her with his words and her father left her to drown.

With her last breath, she cursed Shrava.

The betrayal of her lover was beyond her comprehension. She cursed his line. Cursed everything and everyone he would touch. Cursed herself forever trusting him.

'I would have loved you,' she cried as the sea rushed in around her.

'I would have been yours. And one day I will have vengeance, even if it takes forever. I'll wait in the land beneath the waves. The sea will take you too. It will take all your menfolk, and all who stand with you, and leave your women weeping. Until the day you save my city until you give your all to protect Mû, I curse you and yours to drown.'

The cold hand of death took her, even as she raged, even as she cursed, even as she poured every last ounce of power into her words.

She looked into the face of Yama, the Servant of Death, who had loved her and left her, who would do anything for her. She cried for her lost city, her lost love, her shattered dreams, and he took pity on her, releasing her.

The water took her and made her its bride.

The silence broke into the depths.

No life was left.

Everything was trapped in oblivion for millions of years to come.

6

Jonas

"The state exists for the individual, not the individual for the state! The state must always stand in defence of its people!" Jonas repeated recurrently.

At such moments, he did not notice anything around. To his surprise, he noted that being by the sea positively affected the course of his thinking and helped streamline his thoughts for his research.

After the first three days of rest, during his

morning walks along the coast, he wrote down more in his notebook than he did during the entire year.

After his walk, Jonas would make himself a breakfast of fresh papaya, toast, and tea. Jonas began to get used to the new way of life; he caught himself on the fact that he even likes to spend time in this way - breathing in the beautiful sea air and enjoying the serene sound of the waves.

One morning he woke up in a wonderful mood with a sense of peace and grace.

Early morning's break was blinding with a radiant flooding sun, bathing the endless expanse of the sea; the rays tinted the sky golden and, reflecting off the water, seemed to stare straight into Jonas' soul.

He felt an amazing lightness and self-confidence. Something gave him strength, energy, and inspiration; thoughts became clear and understandable. At that moment, he wanted to create and move further and further, to go forward - straight to his goal, without stopping.

The sea was completely calm. It was so quiet that Jonas stepped forward carefully and lightly as if afraid to hurt and violate the moment's fragile beauty. The coolness of the morning gave lightness to the mind and put everything in its place. At moments like these, people often realize the beauty of life, and Jonas had gained confidence in his judgment.

"Inequality can be defeated," he declared with confidence to himself."

He sincerely began to believe that humanity could defeat crime and poverty. Deep in contemplation, he did not notice that he had left the hotel grounds. Not noticing anything happening, he confidently walked along the seashore, leaving the serviced apartment far behind. A beautiful, mysterious silence, a distant horizon adorned with the sun's rays, finally gave him what he had been looking for - inspiration.

Suddenly, Jonas' attention was drawn to a large rock. He slowed down. The basaltic boulder's unusual colour and shape created the impression of a fantastic unearthly creature that was about to peek out of the ground. He walked slowly towards the rock. It was black and speckled with many white spots. They must be salt crystals, Jonas thought. He touched the stone with his hand, and it seemed to respond to his touch with a quiver. He quickly pulled his hand away and turned around, feeling a chill run down his spine as he only now noticed how far he had gone from the hotel. A feeling of uneasiness took possession of him. It could be dangerous here, Jonas thought and looked around.

A few feet away, a fisherman stood by the water, closely following the fishing rod. Seeing that he was not alone on the coast, Jonas breathed a sigh of relief. He confidently walked towards the fisherman. Wanting to find a more or less acceptable walking path among the rocky shore, Jonas decided to go around a large stone.

Doing so, for some time, he lost sight of where the fisherman was. He heard only water splashes as if a large fish suddenly was at the surface.

"The fisherman must have caught something," he thought and quickened his pace. Far eager to see the huge prey as soon as possible. Getting to the spot, he found to his surprise that the fisherman was gone! Only light waves swayed the float from his fishing rod in clear, transparent water.

Jonas stopped in complete confusion, not understanding anything. "It's strange," he frowned, feeling the anxiety return to him with renewed vigour.

"Maybe he went somewhere? But how come? I have not wandered so far."

He looked around several times, but the fisherman was nowhere to be found. Jonas squinted his eyes and peered into the shallow wavelets of the lagoon.

'Maybe he fell into the water,' he thought. 'But it's very shallow here, and he was standing by the shore.' he muttered to himself, brushing aside the strange thoughts that filled his mind. He shook his head and looked at the calm sea. He heard a strange noise, quickly turned, and looked around.

'Where does this sound come from?'.

At first, the sounds seemed like the splattering of rain, then suddenly he recognized music coming straight from the depths of the sea. This amazing, sweet melody was somewhat reminiscent of a lullaby that his mother sang to him when he was a little boy. Jonas listened carefully. The music notes were coming out of the water more and more clearly, and with every second, they were getting louder and louder.

He distinctly heard the notes of a harp. Before his eyes was a translucent blue azure sky merged with the reflections and the clear straight horizon. The music seemed to beckon him to the depths. Time froze. Without realizing it, he started advancing in the water.

By now, he reached up to his waist. It called him to itself with an unimaginable pull. The melody sunk into Jonas' soul. Everything that had ever bothered him seemed to dwindle into oblivion. All that mattered was that he reached where the music was coming from, he could feel the cool water wrapping around him.

'Stop! Stop!' someone suddenly screamed. 'Don't go further!'

Jonas stopped and turned around, fixing his blank gaze behind him. A man stood on the shore and called him. The beautiful music stopped at once. Jonas woke up from his torpor and could not believe his own eyes - he was right in his clothes, standing waist-deep in water. His notebook, in which he wrote down important thoughts half an hour ago, was now floating in the water not far from the abandoned fishing rod of the disappeared fisherman.

'It can't be... How did this happen?'

He lunged into a couple of movements, caught his floating notebook, clutched it tightly in his palm as

 if it were the last source of sanity, and hurriedly strode ashore.

Completely bewildered, Jonas stopped on the shore when the sand got gritty and looked at the stranger who called him.

The man looked to be middle-aged with an untidy appearance: long hair, an unkempt beard, and a dark sunburnt tan. His deep black eyes stared at Jonas intensely. It was the look of a nervous, mentally distressed person. On the stranger's neck and hands, Jonas noticed deep scars.

'Y... you ...You,' stammered Jonas, 'Did you fish here?'

'No," the stranger gave him an unfriendly look, "Go back to the hotel, *Missier*. Someone like you doesn't belong here. You cannot walk alone in these places, and even more so, go into the water. Go away!'

Despite his accent, he spoke good English.

'What does "like me" mean?' asked Jonas.

"Where's that fisherman?" What's going on here? I don't remember how I got into the water at all, did you see me going in?'

"Yes mister, I saw you walking in the water.... And I knew!'

'What did you know?'

'Go to your hotel *Missier*,' the man told him calmly. "It's dangerous here."

'Dangerous?' Jonas asked.

'The fisherman is gone; he can't be brought back. And you, too, would be missing if it was not for me. You don't have to say thank you, just leave. By doing this, you'll help yourself and me.'

With these prophetic words, the man turned his back on Jonas and slowly walked away.

Jonas was confused but followed the man's instructions. He made his way to his apartment, this time his steps were not that relaxed. He wanted to be on the housing grounds, see people around him, and feel safe. A light breeze picked up and sent a light chill to his scorched skin.

'What just happened?' He pondered, bewildered.

Jonas went straight to the shower; he came out fresh and free from the sticky saltwater and gritty sand. The fine sand is good to walk on when dry, but when wet it was a real nightmare to shake off. He made himself a refreshing cup of tea and sat down on the balcony with a sea view.

He always gasped each time he saw the stunning colour of the lagoon.

But not today. He thought something more sinister was lurking underneath all that beauty. He was lucky to have been saved in the nick of time.

What if that man had not been here?

On one side, his curious mind was drawn towards wanting to know what was out there. But for now, he was glad to be alive and having tea in safety. Life could not have been simpler.

On the surface, that is.

7

Inspector Sanjiv

'Madame, you will kill anybody who eats that!' Nina gasped.

Ah Cheew continued shaking drops of chili oil into the spicy soy sauce she was stirring.

'Just a bit more. Just for flavouring,' she said.

'This oil is not too hot. I read some more about the dead woman.'

Ah Cheew was working on a new line of chili oils with her signature pickle with garlic chives. Glass jars containing a variety of thinly sliced chili peppers fried in different oils lined the kitchen counters.

'Ayo assez do, madame. Dimoune so vente pou enflamé sa.' You shouldn't make it so hot, people's tummies would be upset.

'If you want hot, you should try the one I made with my *naga* king chili,' Ah Cheew said.

She had started growing imported chili plants in her garden to see how they did in Mauritius. The *pima petar* was not hot enough for her taste. She had gotten used to their heat and found them rather bland.

The humid climate seems to suit the Naga jholokia king chili, reputed to be the hottest chili in the world, and Ah Cheew had just bottled her first harvest. The heat of the tiny Rodriguan chilli was no longer enough for her palate.

'The *naga* king chili is so hot that the Indian army is trying to use it as a weapon! In tear gas and hand grenades! And you want to feed that to customers? *'Sa pou ale assize l'hôpital sa.* If they all die, who will buy your food?'

'In a warm country, you need hot food. Besides, if it is so hot, you only need to use a few drops each time, one bottle will last a long time, good value for money!"

'Your sense of economy baffles me. How are you going to make money if you sell them one bottle and they don't need to come back for years? You should be like the iPhone - every year you must upgrade!'

Ah Cheew did not like criticism which put a nail to her logic. So, she spoke randomly but paid no heed to the caution of Nina.

Inspector Sanjiv was having lunch at Ah Cheew's joint today. Mopping his curry with a piece of roti, he also kept an eye on Nina. The young woman looked beautiful today. She wore a teal green salwar and a matching chiffon *horni* over her head. Her cheeks were flushed and glowing, from being too close to the stove.

At first, Sanjiv had been taken aback by how Ah Cheew and her maid, Nina, talked to each other, but he soon realized it was a game for them. Like children playing *lastik*, a rubber band stretched and thrown in a circle, the goal was to keep the dialogue going rather than score points.

When Nina was not around, Ah Cheew would talk to one of the photos of her late husband. But that wasn't much fun for the obvious lack of response. She would then wobble her way across the tables trying to chat up customers.

Today, despite Nina being there responding to their game of verbal *lastik*, Ah Cheew picked up her stick and came out of the counter. She greeted a few regulars and made her way towards Sanjiv. The latter waited for what she had to tell him. Because most times, that's what the customers did. She talked, they nodded, and continued eating. They all had a very limited time for lunch break, and they made sure they didn't lose any precious time in the banter of Ah Cheew.

'So, how is our Inspector doing today? All good? How is the curry? Did Nina give you a good serving?'

There could have been no better answer to this string of questions but a wave from his left unused hand, in acknowledgment that all was good.

'I see that you are mopping the sauce well, which means it is good. And I like you eating with your hand. Many customers use a fork and knife to eat a roti which is abhorrent.'

'I like it that way'

'Good! Tell me Inspector, how is that investigation of the murder going. You know … the French woman whose body was found …? Sanjiv wiped his mouth and looked at Ah Cheew with no surprise.

'I guess good … all good, yes' was a dry cautious reply from the Inspector.

But this wasn't enough for Ah Cheew, she wanted to know every detail. The questions were jumping in her stomach like corn popping in a hot pot.

'I heard it was a woman … Who was she? How horrible! Who could have killed her and why? Oh God, why?'

Sanjiv thought quickly about how and what to say. Ah Cheew's eyes twinkled with eagerness and she waited for the answers with a large smile. As if this would charm the man to give out all the secrets he knew.

'Uh … the investigation is on, we are working

hard on the case, but I am bound by law not to disclose anything, you will know in time when we are ready.'

'Hmmm... alright! Don't hesitate to come around for lunch, Nina always looks forward to seeing you. She holds you in great esteem you know?' Ah, Cheew was using her last dice to try to gain the inspector's confidence, who had turned as mute as a carp.

'Really?' Sanjiv half got up from his seat.

'You know, women don't show their feelings openly. Besides, you know, she has to be cautious.'

This did the trick. Sanjiv moved towards Ah Cheew and whispered 'She was a foreigner, a professor, that's all I can say, it did not come from me, remember'

'I never heard anything ... take it from me'

whispered back a delighted Ah Cheew.

Above the worktop along the right-hand wall a row of white cupboards stands out, reflecting fading daylight onto the small drop-leaf table in the centre of the kitchen, and the large plastic dustbin, full to the brim with white basmati rice, in the corner facing the door.

Nina was trying to catch a large pot to wash rice before it went on the stove for cooking when she felt Ah Cheew's presence by her side. She beamed with happiness and pulled Nina by the arm. A rare gesture to show her utter impatience.

She was burning to tell Nina something.

'What did I tell you? Aren't I clever?'

Nina glanced at her and nodded. Always best to make Ah Cheew happy when she is in this state.

'Your inspector Sanjiv told me ...'

'My inspector ... since when he is my inspector?!" Rebuked a miffed Nina, her two hands sat squarely on her hips.

This suggested familiarity with her boss was most displeasing to her. Ah Cheew lost her countenance for a split second in front of this reaction from the young woman.

"But I was only suggesting something positive ... what's wrong with that? Why do you always have to charge at me like a *Mama Kali*?"

"Oh yes! *Mama Kali* and why not? What's wrong with that? Tomorrow you will marry us, and next week, you will be looking for names for our children!"

"Of course, I wish you to be happy *...to bien ingrate selma!*"

"I am not interested in Mr Sanjiv."

"And why not? He is a good-looking man, respectable and a high-ranking officer in the police force, what are you expecting to find... nobility?"

"No, I am not looking for anyone. Can you please stop matchmaking for me, Madame?"

"Listen, silly girl! ... what's most important is that Inspector Sanjiv has given me more inside information about the body!" Ah Cheew rubbed her hands gleefully.

She drew closer to Nina, and the latter retreated to the sink, washing the rice under the tap. Three rinses, that's what Ah Cheew taught her to do for cooking fluffy rice. The main starch needs to get dislodged from the grains of rice and to keep a good knuckle deep of water to avoid stodginess. Her boss is engrossed in this murder thing, and for some reason, it's good for Nina. She can get some freedom to advance her skills in the kitchen. With Ah Cheew hovering around her, it is not always easy.

"I am always trying to help you, Nina, is that not what I have done so far?' The droopy puppy eyes of Ah Cheew were staring at Nina and the latter turned her gaze away. Better not give in to her antics, once again. However, it's true that without the help of Ah Cheew, she wouldn't have been where she is now.

Ah Cheew had retreated to her seat behind the counter. She had plunged her flat face into the Chinese newspaper, reading about Madame Kwon's predictions. Her sure escape crowns her utter frustration, when she is sulking. The Astrologer's predictions would interest her, as per her moods.

Today, it seemed that the reading wasn't good. She flung the paper to the side while giving a frowning glance to Nina. There are days when she simply cannot understand the young maid's wrath against her, she is just ungrateful.

8

Gululethu

Fabio Grignon spent the rest of the morning at an Italian restaurant.

A solid refuge to feel grounded after heavy jet lag. He has been sent on a mission following an order for an inquest by the French Embassy about the disappearance of Professor Valériane Ducasse. Fabio was born and brought up in Paris by his French-Italian parents, but his allegiance to food was very much on his maternal side. Italian mothers hold food and their families close to their hearts. At first, he was enchanted to learn that he was being sent on a mission to Île Maurice. Who wouldn't? The exotic tropical island was known for its round-the-year sunshine and gorgeous turquoise and crystal-clear lagoons.

But since his arrival, he had had two meetings at the central CID office in an old stone building called the Line Barracks. The horror of the crime only rang to him in its seriousness when he went through the pictures of the disfigured body.

He was eager to finish the meeting and rush to a place where he could catch his breath again. One kind police officer guided him to this restaurant after he inquired about his Italian-sounding name. He was glad he reached this place. The restaurant was housed in an old French colonial house and smelled of freshly cooked foods. The animated crowd was the tell-tale sign of a good eating joint.

It had a main atrium, and was roomy, with a floor-to-ceiling saltwater aquarium full of tropical fish and live coral that wrapped halfway around the curving walls. A breeze flowing in from open windows from the facing harbour did a better job of cooling the place than the slow-turning ceiling fans.

Fabio made three trips to the buffet table, stacking his plate high with toast, eggs, sausages, home fries, bacon, pastries, pancakes, and exotic fruit. Dead bodies always made him hungrier than usual, as if excessive eating were necessary to remind him that he was still among the living. His beach hut was a twenty-minute walk on meandering brick and stone walkways. He had hoped for an entry-level penthouse suite with a personal butler. So far, the best thing about it was having a beach hut reserved for his entire stay, complete with a well-stocked cooler, an afternoon cocktail of the day, and food service just a phone call away. That was his share of luxury in this famous tropical paradise.

When he arrived at his beach hut, which looked like a giant cocktail umbrella with its wooden pillar and thatched roof, Manoj, the resort's guest relation's officer, was draping blue towels over two lounge chairs.

"Hello, Mr. Fabio."

He greeted him with a firm handshake. Fabio shook his dark tanned hand. He guided him through the room and the amenities and left with a smile. That warmth is legendary of Mauritians who have carved themselves quite an enviable spot under the sun in the world hospitality scene.

Fabio settled down in his new working environment, thinking, if only it wasn't for such a sinister reason, this would be a perfect vacation.

*

The sun was at its zenith. Scorching heat and blaring white light flooded everything out in the open. With his back to the door, Inspector Sanjiv scooped his Ray-Bans off his belt with an agility Fabio could only envy.

"Regarding the woman, do you know if the authorities have started an inquiry?"

"Yes. Dead white women always draw more attention than their exotic counterparts, even in places where they are the minority."

Fabio didn't quite know what to make of this queer statement, but he was ready to learn about each and every way the local folks lived. After all, he had just arrived. Assuming the Inspector was right and the woman was a tourist, Fabio doubted race played a role in the strong law enforcement response.

This was an island dependent on the almighty tourist dollar, and any dead tourist was bad for business.

"Now the staff must tread lightly. The French embassy will be displeased and inconvenienced by an inquiry."

Fabio glanced at his watch.

"*Ah mince*! I'm running late. *Désolé je dois filer.*"

As he hustled off to the beach, Inspector Sanjiv turned back to the cooler and pulled out a chilled Sprite. He had met the French investigator in his usual haunt at Ah Cheew's restaurant. Probably, because he felt a bit more confident there, seeing Nina. Ah Cheew had not left him out of her visual range, although from a distance, her eyes seemingly looked closed. But Inspector Sanjiv knows how alert she is, upon watching anyone with a police uniform venturing from the station to her eatery.

Tega came back after a few days. However, no matter how hard he tried, he failed to garner a crowd around him to listen to his stories.

'Bonzour Madame Ah Cheew, ki manière? Tou korek?'

'Bonzour Tega, apar douler tou korek...dire mwa oune gagne nouvel?'

'Ki nouvel?'

Ah Cheew made sure she told Tega about her new information, gathered incognito from Inspector Sanjiv. Seeing the conversation from where he was sitting, Sanjiv reckoned it could only be about the murder. He decided to get up and leave. Nina glanced towards him and gave a faint shy smile. The Inspector's heart skipped a beat. He surely was smitten by the young woman. Sadly, his romance seemed to be going at snail's speed. Without Ah Cheew he wouldn't even have guessed that Nina was also attracted to him. He needed to work upon this matter, but for now, he had better hasten to fill in his log after meeting Fabio. He picked his *képi* and left.

*

The harsh Mauritius summer sun beat down mercilessly upon them, doubly cruel as it reflected off the water's shimmering surface into their squinting eyes, stinging with sweat. The pounding of deep-throated kettle drums quickened their cadence. The slaves strained against their oars to avoid the stinging lash and the pouring of salt water on their already scarred and sunburned backs. With a single man to each oar, they had been trained to keep in perfect rhythm and pull together as one. Turning their vessel into the most lethal weapon anywhere on the Great Sea. The galley master shouted out the closing of the distance periodically in between drum beats. He didn't want them to exhaust themselves as they surged toward a target, they couldn't see. Best to always save a small reserve of strength for the final push, soon to come. Here and there the most weakened of the slaves slumped at their oar, their hearts bursting from the strain, or the meagre rations and ill treatment will finally take its ultimate toll. Since they were shackled to one another and to the floorboards of the galley, there was no time to throw their limp bodies overboard in the heat of battle. Instead, their oar was simply tossed away from the ship, so as not to interfere with the rest still pumping frantically in unison. Woe be it that any surviving slave with no oar after the battle had been won.

And if the battle was lost, what did it matter?

Their ship would burn or sink, their chains ensuring a trip to the bottom, along with their brethren. Such was the life of a slave upon a fighting galley. Christian Dupont subconsciously smiled his approval as he watched the chase from afar on his flag ship. Commander of the great fleet, he was thick-muscled with a broad, powerful chest, and could still be easily mistaken for the elite filibusters he led.

His skin was bronzed from the sun and sea just like the armour he wore, the crow's feet at the edges of eyes betraying his years spent at sea. He now battled victoriously with his leadership and sharp intellect.

Here, they had cleverly lured the last of the pirates from their lair with a fat, slow moving merchant vessel that had proven irresistible. Christian had devised the grand strategy that ensured the same choreographed act was played out up and down the coasts. All around the scattered island anchorages known to be favourite haunts of the scourge of these pirates. What made the ploy deadly efficient was the genius of its simplicity. All done before a word of warning could be passed from one pirate haven to the next. He tilted his head, and could hear the collision of wooden ships, even here. The sound carried across the water on the slightest breath of a breeze, unequivocally destructive. The omens were good, and sporadic plumes of bright-coloured liquid stone and smoke were tossed skyward from his lair deep within the very earth itself.

Surely, this was signalling accolades for these masters of the sea. As the wind picked up, the fleet sailed onward without the aid of oars, the slaves catching their collective breath. They were reorganized to balance the remaining manpower. Their dead comrades were unshackled and unceremoniously dumped into the passing waves, where dorsal fins below and scavenger birds above fought one another for their feast.

For a change, the slaves could watch vengeance meted out upon someone else, now in the form of the dazed and newly captive pirates. But that didn't always bring solace. Vengeance burned deep within the soul of each slave, their callused hands bleeding and full of splinters, their ankles rubbed raw by the shackles, the sharp bones of their buttocks nearly breaking through their emaciated skin on the rough benches of the galley. Perhaps retribution wouldn't happen in their own fleeting lifetimes. But they prayed it would ultimately come down upon their oppressors with fury, and avenge their tormented souls.

The breezes continued to favour the journey, and soon the great port of Grand Port loomed in the distance. The slaves limbered up, believing they would have to row the galley into its berth. But no order was given, and they drifted beyond the reefs for two full days. The crew celebrated and drank rum, making sport of torturing the injured and oldest of the captives before throwing them overboard, while abusing the women their commanders gave them. They lusted for the rare times when all captured women were fair game, regardless of rank.

Almost by the hour more and more ships gathered further away, slowly drifting around the flag ship. Christian held counsel with each captain, and waited until he felt he had gathered enough of the great fleet to properly impress the king. He then organized a procession into the vast, concentric harbour.

His ship was proudly at the vanguard as they slowly entered the port, looking up at the magnificent Montagne Lion, below which sat the sleepy town of Mahebourg.

As they approached the port, the clanging of bells and cymbals and thumping of drums could be heard all around. He was a man at the pinnacle of his powers, self-confident in the way of men accustomed to accomplishing great things, forged by continually overcoming great adversity. He came from a seafaring nation at the country's peninsula jutting its cliffs into the Atlantic.

The reach of the empire was fast growing. It was reaching out to the edges of the unknown world, and pushing its boundaries beyond it. Spices and gold were the main captured bounty.

The pirates hidden along mainland coves and backwater islands had become an increasing menace to the free flow of goods. Christian had aggressively pursued them to their lairs and made bloody spectacles of their leaders, the wounded, and the weak. The slave markets were now bursting with young men with strong backs, and well-built women with glistening skin. Proud and defiant, they were independent and unbowed, even in their bondage - which made them even more attractive to their greedy masters. Christian was given a gift of one such captured slave by the chieftains of the slave traders.

He was an Omani who told him that he claimed an exquisite beauty from the last ravaged village near the coast of Pemba.

Tall, raven haired, and graceful, she had stood out of the chaos and carnage with her quiet, unassuming dignity. She would soon need to teach her proper place among her betters.

But for now, Christian smiled at the nights of carnal pleasure awaiting him once on shore. His captured gift was indeed a sight to behold.

*

Slavery has been an important phenomenon throughout history. It has been found in many places, from classical antiquity to very recent times. Africa has been intimately connected with this history, both as a major source of slaves for ancient civilizations, the Islamic world, India, and the Americas, and as one of the principal areas where slavery was common.

Indeed, in Africa, slavery lasted well into the twentieth century – notably longer than in the Americas. Such antiquity and persistence require explanation, both to understand the historical development of slavery in Africa in its own right and to evaluate the relative importance of the slave trade to this development. Broadly speaking, slavery expanded in at least three stages – 1350 to 1600, 1600 to 1800, and 1800 to 1900 – by which time slavery had become a fundamental feature of the African political economy. This expansion occurred on two levels that were linked to the external slave trade. First, slavery became more common over an increasingly greater geographical area, spreading outward from those places that participated directly in the external slave trade. Second, the role of slaves in the economy and society became more important, resulting in the transformation of the social, economic, and political order. Again, the external trade was associated with this transformation.

Slavery is one form of exploitation. Its special characteristics include the idea that slaves are property; that they are outsiders who are alien by origin or who are denied their heritage through judicial or other sanctions; that coercion can be used at will; that their labour is at the complete disposal of a master; that they do not have the right to their own sexuality and, by extension, to their own reproductive capacities; and that the slave status is inherited unless provision is made to ameliorate that status. These various attributes need to be examined in greater detail to clarify the distinctions between slavery and other servile relationships. As property, slaves are considered to be chattel, which is to say they can be bought and sold.

Slaves belong to their masters who, at least theoretically, have complete power over them. Religious institutions, kinship units, and other groups in the same society do not protect slaves as legal persons, even though the fact that slaves are also human beings, has sometimes been recognized. Because they are considered chattel, slaves can be treated as commodities. But slaves seldom have been merely commodities, and often restrictions have been placed on the sale of slaves once some degree of acculturation has taken place. These restrictions could be purely moral, as they were in the Americas, where, at least in theory, it was thought wrong to divide families when sales were taking place, although in fact slave owners did whatever they wanted. In other situations, restrictions were actually enforced, or persons were automatically granted some degree of emancipation that precluded sale. In Islamic practice and under Islamic law, women taken as concubines could not be legally sold once they had given birth to children by their master. Furthermore, such children were technically free and usually recognized as such. The women became legally free on the death of their master in many cases, and in some they were nominally free as soon as they gave birth, although they could not normally terminate their status as concubines. In reality, they attained an intermediate position between slaves and free. Other restrictions on sale limited the ability of masters to sell the children of slaves, either because of religious sentiments, in the case of Islam, or because an acceptable kinship or ethnic status had been confirmed. If a sale did take place, it was carefully justified in terms of criminal activity, sorcery, or some other ideologically acceptable reason; often these same reasons could result in the sale of freeborn members of the same society. Nonetheless, it is characteristic of slavery that the slave is considered property of another person or some corporate group, despite restrictions on the nature of this relationship that developed in actual situations. A digression is necessary to establish what is meant by "freedom." The term is really relative. People are either more or less free to make decisions for themselves. All societies place numerous constraints on individuals, but even when this is recognized, we can still understand slaves as people who are particularly 'unfree'. In the context of slave societies, freedom involved a recognized status in a caste, a ruling class, a kinship group, or some such body. Such identification included a bundle of rights and obligations that varied considerably with the situation but were still distinct from those for slaves, who technically had no rights, only obligations. The act of emancipation, when it existed, conveyed recognition that slave and free were not the same. Emancipation dramatically demonstrated that power was in the hands of the free, not the slaves.

*

Gugulethu sat unmoving in the chamber, unsure what fate held for her. After bathing her, a young slave girl methodically brushed her hair out, then trimmed the edges to match the style favoured by the island's women. Dark kohl made from the soot of an oil lamp was applied around her eyes, and a mirror held to her face so she could approve. Gugulethu was startled, having never seen a mirror. The only reflection of her own image she had ever beheld was from gazing into ponds near her home, or the water pots she filled. Her name meant 'our treasure, our pride' often said by her mother while doing her plaits. But as a little girl, she had no idea what beauty she blossomed into, attracting the cursed eyes of the chieftain from the tribe on the other side of the lake.

She had never seen anything like this, an image so vivid and full of colour. She couldn't suppress a smile as she stared at her own delicate features framed by thick curls of black hair, and felt at the smooth dark olive-coloured skin of her face.

 It was all so unreal to her. She tried to communicate with the girl, whose dark, nearly black skin, betrayed an abduction from a distant land. The slave spoke the language of the islanders haltingly, she was still learning it. But Creole was somehow how her own native mother tongue sounded. When she was finally able to make herself understood, the slave put a finger to her lips, only to whisper. Gugulethu pondered her predicament and sighed. She would never see her family again. Nor her love, Amati. If he had even survived when his ship was boarded. What could have possibly become of him? Will I ever know?

She started sobbing, the tears running freely and ruining her make-up. The slave girl motioned her to be quiet and still, and patiently cleaned and reapplied it.

Gululethu reflected back on her abduction. It had all been so disorienting, the leather clad soldiers spilling upon the shores of her little village, while she stood trembling on the dock. A man of rank saw her and pulled her aside, while other women were taken into bondage or abused at the whims of the rampaging warriors. Anyone not thought to make a worthy slave was immediately put to the sword. Only a few old women were left alive when the ships departed. They were spared not out of mercy, but to tell the tale and spread fear. A warning of what became of those who defied the new masters and harboured filibusters. When Gululethu had been towed away, an image was burnt into her memory: that of the village going up in flames, smoke curling high in the air, vultures descending to feast upon the scattered bodies of her kinfolk. An entire way of life lain waste.

The slave girl put a finger under Gululethu's chin, bringing her back to the present. She made her look up, and seemed to glimpse into her very soul.

"You beautiful, you are their colour. Someone important take you. Be submissive, not proud."

The slave pulled her clothing aside to reveal her back.

"Proud brings pain, proud makes scars."

Gululethu looked away, about to burst into tears again. The slave grabbed her by both shoulders, and shook her with surprising strength.

"Be strong. Forget home now. Home dead for me, dead for you. You endure. Survive."

Gululethu composed herself, managed a smile, and put the girl's hands in hers. There was a look of gratitude and an unspoken thank you on her lips. She felt her chair rock slightly, and thought she was being pulled closer by the slave girl.

But her hands weren't on the chair, they were in hers. A cat that had been asleep in the corner awoke, growled, then darted out of the door.

A panicked flock of birds from the

waterfront flew overhead, screeching loudly. A cup fell from the table near the window, as they looked at one another, confused. The earth trembled, lightly at first, then with more force. Pottery fell and broke, chairs overturned, startled animals cried out. They instinctively ran out into the street, away from the pieces of rock and mortar falling off the facings of the citadel's walls. A small crowd gathered, no one knew where it was safe. Overseers appeared at intersections to ensure no slaves ran away in the chaos.

'Where would I even run to? Gululethu thought. 'There is nowhere to go. This is all the land of my enemies.'

Small scattered cracks appeared in the street, noxious fumes seeping upward and assaulting their senses. The slave girl grabbed Gululethu's hand and pointed to the mountain overlooking Mahebourg. A plume of smoke had arisen from it, which was drifting with the wind. Towards them, and the docks just below. Small bits of stone started hitting her upturned face, pattering down like hail. They started increasing in size, stinging when they hit.

The crowd, which had been mostly silent in awe of the spectacle, began to panic. People started screaming, running aimlessly about. There was no escape from the increasing fumes or the pummelling of airborne stones. Fires broke out from unattended hearths and toppled lamps, adding to the confusion and turmoil.

The sharp crack of a whip instinctively made Gululethu turn her head. The crowd parted, two columns of soldiers briskly trotting through, then pausing. An imposing looking man in their midst, dressed in impressive battle regalia, took charge. He called to the overseers, and directed the male slaves be formed into lines from the fountains to the fires. Clay vessels were found, and water was passed hand to hand to douse the flames. Gululethu recognized him, he was the very same leader of the armada that had brought with her and the surviving villagers as bounty. She briefly caught his eye, and he bowed his head toward her. He then deployed a few men, shouted instructions, and led the rest of the soldiers down to the docks, to the great ships.

"Put your backs into it or I'll make an offering of you," a slave driver yelled, cracking his whip on a hapless man who had dropped a heavy, slippery pot of water. Gululethu could deduce most of his words, and the tone of his voice made the meaning perfectly clear.

The line of slaves passing water pots fell into

a rhythm. One by one the scattered fires were extinguished. After a few minutes, the cloud above dissipated and the stones stopped raining down. The male slaves were marched off, while the women slaves were herded together until their owners could come for them.

By dusk, Gululethu and the young slave girl were claimed, taken back to the house, and put to work cleaning up. In the morning she was made to sit again, and her hair was tended to and make-up reapplied. She was puzzled why such attention was paid to her, until there was a knock at the door and two soldiers entered.

They signalled Gululethu to come with them. She arose hesitantly, unsure of what fate awaited her. The slave girl ran to her and hugged her, whispering into her ear.

"We survivors, you and I. We will meet again, in the fields."

Gululethu embraced her hard, trying to hold back the tears.

"Yes, someday, but not until we do great deeds to earn our entry."

Gululethu was guided down the main thoroughfare to the crowded docks, and gazed at the massive ships around the harbour.

They worked their way through gangs of slaves loading the ships with provisions and trade goods, soldiers shouting directions, gulls diving for scraps, a cacophony of noise around them. They stopped in front of the largest ship in the harbour, prominent due to the great flag bearing the symbols of the golden land of the masters fluttering above it in the breeze. It was emblazoned with a figure of a mermaid, with flowing hair gazing ahead.

Gululethu was led aboard by her escort. She heard whistles and catcalls, not realizing they were directed at her. A figure emerged from the far side of the galley and all noise ceased.

Men came to attention, the crowded deck parting as Gululethu came across. The commander of the great fleet walked directly over to her, and put his arm out. "My name is Christian DuPont, Commander in Chief. You will personally attend to me. Welcome on board."

The young slave didn't know that her fate would mirror that of millions caught in the same greedy trade of men within the same ocean, eras later, which were never known nor recorded in history.

Months of sailing and consequent day and night serving the captain, broke Gululethu to the bone. Her spirit soared high to the sky when she was asleep finally after the sexual assaults of the man who 'owned' her.

It cried out 'freedom' to the Creator.

It summoned the spirit of the universe to take her life. But they all remained silent. As if they all conjured together so that she led such a life of misery.

One day, the ship moored to a lagoon. All the sailors were busy unloading empty barrels and crates to restock. Gululethu couldn't recognise the land. She looked for a clue that it could be the island where she was taken to, but no, it wasn't. She joined the other women and helped in gathering foods and drinks. The days went on, she counted five where the moon was waning. One opportunity presented itself.

*

It was a dark night and Gululethu was running.

Branches tore at her skin. Birds, screeching, took flight at the pounding of her strides. The ground was muddy and uneven, slick with the residue of recent rains, and she slipped, falling hard against the rough bark of a palm tree. She slid down to the soil, to where ants marched, beetles scurried and unseen worms burrowed through the earth. With ragged breaths she gulped the heavy, humid air into her lungs. She could taste its dampness on her tongue, tinged with the acidic bite of her own fear.

What had she done? She looked behind her. Looming in the darkness was the outline of the low hill where they were camping, its arms splayed out like four sharp-edged daggers marking an angry cross in the sky. Terror clawed at her throat, as if the hill itself had eyes and could whisper to the overseer what it had seen. It was not too late. She could still climb back over the wall and creep through the fields of half-planted cane, where gaping holes awaited young green stalks. She could return to her hut, one wooden square among many, and lie back on the sleeping mat that was worn thin from years of use. She could wait for dawn and another day of labour . . .

Scrambling to her feet, she kept running. Her legs plunged her deeper into the half-formed shadows of the forest. Her chest ached. She wanted to collapse, but could not; her body, unbidden, carried her further and further away from the camp. Every snap of a twig sounded like a gunshot; the murmuring of cane toads became the distant cries of searching men. She must keep running. Alone, mud-streaked, with weariness sinking into her very bones, a question haunted her – was this freedom? The empty forest.

Her fleeing, sick with dread. Was this what they had hoped for, all along?

The day before, all the slaves of the camp and the neighbouring plantation had gathered outside the grand mansion.

A stone-faced set of white people waited for them. The master, on horseback, flanked by the sirdar, with the master's wife and three children standing on the steps of the house. The white people stared at the slaves. The slaves stared back. They all knew what was coming. Some of the slaves even smiled. Gululethu was among those who didn't. She was old enough to remember other times when there were whispers about the end of slavery. She would not believe it until she heard it for herself from the master's own mouth. The master's balding forehead glistened with sweat in the heat.

As he brought his horse forward, Gululethu caught a glimpse of his wife's face, her lips pressed into a line of seething contempt. It was this sight, more than anything, that strengthened Gululethu's resolve. She dared to hope.

Somehow, the captain appeared only at night to take Gululethu to hell again and again. He disappeared before the early morning rays' hit the hut's door covered by a gunny curtain tied by coir ropes. Then, the captain stopped coming. The Master then said that the King had decreed an end to slavery.

As of the following day, the new Emancipation Act would come into effect. They were free. Some people cried. Others yelled and danced in delight. They were a mass of shouting, sweating bodies, a river bursting its banks. The master and the overseer barked useless orders, unable to be heard over the noise. Eventually, the master rode his horse through the crowd at a gallop, just to get them quiet again. Its hooves kicked one woman's head in, and she died instantly. But she died free.

There was more, the master said. They were no longer slaves, but they were instead his apprentices. By law, they would work for him for six years. They could not leave. When the sun rose, Gululethu and all the rest would be going back out to finish the planting. They would tend to the cane until the next harvest, and the harvest after. Six years of cutting and planting and cutting again.

Freedom was just another name for the life they had always lived.

An ugly hiss went through the crowd. The overseer swung his whip slung over his shoulder, reaching to bring it down. A hundred pairs of eyes watched the arc of his hand. The master's horse blew air through its nostrils, its reins pulled taut. The hiss died, and the crowd was still.

Gululethu heard the news of hollow freedom in silence. For years, she had lived in perpetual twilight. Her life had shrunk to the size of the plantation, the routine of endless toil, and the long shadows of what had once been.

Freedom was an emptiness that could only be filled with sugar cane.

That night, everything was the same. The press of the ground on her back. The shape of her limbs, thin and knotted with sinew. The musty smell of her hut. Days of labour lay ahead, her life as neatly ploughed as the furrows in the field. In sleep, she dreamt of her mother. Or, maybe it was the idea of a mother, an outline of warmth and kindness. She couldn't remember her own mother. The mother was there in front of her, but somehow the young slave knew that she was also not there.

She was somewhere far across the sea. She was fragile, a wisp of smoke. She could not stay long. The mother spoke a name, and Gululethu knew that it was her name – the name she was meant to have before some white man called her something else. What the white man gives, he can always take away. But this other name – this was hers. Gululethu repeated it. The syllables felt strange in her mouth, but as the thrum of speech vibrated through her, they gave her strength. She was able to stand without stooping. She could feel the weight of her body, solid and powerful.

The mother stepped back and began to dissolve, one drop at a time, soaking the earth underneath her. When she was gone, the soil glistened a deep, rich red.

Gululethu had awoken in pitch darkness – wild, trembling, and glistening with sweat – and her body could not be stilled. It moved without her asking it to, it moved on animal instinct alone, crawling out of the hut, unfurling, and flinging itself in the forest,

Gululethu asked herself again: was this freedom?

A violent rupture, a body driven to flight, a mind paralyzed with horror as it watched things unfold beyond its control? The trees had no answer. Their leaves whispered in the wind, and Gululethu imagined them taunting her – What now? Her body moved beyond the range of thought, with a desperate will of its own. She kept running. She had no way to mark the passing of time on that moonless night, but by the burning in her legs Rachel knew she had travelled an hour or more when she heard it.... so, faint she thought she was imagining it at first. Singing.

She saw a glow of light, flickering between the tree trunks. She advanced slowly, her mind filled with thoughts of ghosts and night-time spirits. But as the singing swelled, accompanied by drumming, filling the forest with sound, her fears receded. The noises were joyful and human and drew her in. A clearing. A tight circle of bare earth in between the trees. At its centre, dozens of people were dancing round a crackling fire, with still more lingering at the edge.

As the dancers spun past, Galalethu heard snatches of different words and melodies all blending into one. She heard some French, but also other languages, older languages that spoke not to her ears but to her bones. Gululethu stood in shadow, watching. She had been to dances before, as a younger woman, but not like this. Those dances had always been folded into plantation life. They took place in the slave quarters, or in the market square of a nearby town. At any time, a white passer-by could appear, or the face of the master in a window of the great house, reminding all present that their joy was not boundless; it could not overflow the confines of slavery.

This clearing sparkled with a different kind of magic. With no prying eyes to break the spell, the dancers moved with an unencumbered grace. The insistent pull of the drums drew the young woman closer, closer, into the light. She found herself one body among many, swaying in time to the beat. She began to tap her foot and hum a song of her own. A woman threw out her arm, her eyes wide and white, with glittering circles of firelight at the centre. She seized her by the wrist. She sang the command, her voice low and sweet. 'Dance!' was swept into the throng. In an instant, she lost all sense of herself. She had no end and no beginning, no edges or limits at all. Her whole body dissolved into the rhythm. The dance rippled through the crowd as if through water, and Gululethu gave herself up to the music. Every ache in her body eased. She emptied her lungs of a song she had not even known was inside her. Someone was holding her hand; she reached out and grabbed another's hand, who grabbed another's hand.

As the flames leapt into the sky, Gululethu thought she could see the chain of hands climbing to the heavens, a line of people through time and space, united by a single drumbeat.

When the last embers of the fire died, everyone stopped dancing. The dawn was beginning to break, grey light leaking through the trees, and the rising sun brought an end to whatever magic had bound them together. It suddenly felt cool, the warmth of the fire having lost its power to comfort.

People began to leave, most of them tacking west, dawn breaking on their backs, returning to their plantations. Hovering at the edge of the clearing, standing between two broad oaks, Gululethu wondered if she should follow them. Her absence at the plantation might not yet have been noticed. But she hesitated too long. Soon, everyone was gone and she was alone. She slipped eastwards, back into the forest. All of the running and the dancing weighed her down. She ached everywhere. It forced her to a slow pace. The terror of the first flight had faded to a kind of daze, and she stared up through the canopy at the sky.

Somehow, the darkness had been easier – it had a kernel of mystery to it, a sense that the night held many possible worlds, their boundaries worn thin, so that anyone might pass between them. Sunlight was a reminder of the endless march of one day into the next, the unstoppable passage of time to which Gululethu had been enslaved all her life. Still the question plagued her – What now? It had a weary edge, a hopelessness. Her run from the plantation had been pure survival.

Now, she wandered aimlessly through the undergrowth; there was no path, and she stumbled over exposed roots. Her head throbbed with thirst and her limbs felt like logs attached to her body, but her steps guided themselves. Apart from the soft thud of her feet on the bare earth, the only sounds were the chattering grackles that flitted overhead. She climbed the gentle slope of a hill. When she reached the top, suddenly there was the sea. The sight of its dazzling blue spread below stopped the tired slave in her tracks. She had reached the limits of the island.

The rising sun dipped its lower rays into the water on the horizon. Against the bluish grey sky, the sea was a shocking shade of blue, dappled with white-gold sunlight. She felt a strange sense of being at peace.

All her life, nothing had belonged to her. The sense of belonging was one way. She was owned. With her world boxed in by plantation walls, and its perimeter patrolled by the overseer's whip, it had seemed as if there was nothing the white men did not own. But now, here was the sea.

Vast, defiant and not owned, even white men, could not claim it. However, much they grasped at it, its waters would run through their fingers and plunge back into the depths. At the plantation, Gululethu had always been made to feel small. With the sea spread out in front of her, she felt small in a different way – not small in herself but a small part of everything that surrounded her.

Immersed in the infinite sea. There was freedom in this new kind of smallness, an exhilarating sense that she was in the world, and not just passing through it at a white man's pace. The question came to mind once again – What now?

This time it had a new quality – it looked forward, outwards, across the water. Not back over her shoulder to anyone who might be pursuing her. Her lungs opened; she could breathe again. Her gaze wandered from the horizon down the hill.

At first glance, the hillside was deserted. And yet . . . She leaned forward a little, shielding her eyes against the sun.

Nestled among the trees, about halfway down, she thought she could see a glistening shape emerging from the sea and clambering the rocks nearby. It shone like a jewel.

A spirit?! She had heard that the sea hid in its kingdom more spirits than the human mind could imagine. Could this be one? The young woman closed her tired eyes and thought 'am I dreaming?' But she wasn't, when she opened her eyes, she saw the 'spirit' lifting its head and looking in her direction.

Could it have seen her? Gululethu's heart was knocking against her rib cage like a mad dog wanting to break free. She dunked in the thickets and hid herself better. This wasn't the time to allow herself to be captured again!

Certainly not by a spirit.

9

The Find

« To ascend into heaven, you must first work your way through the seven levels of purgatory. Pride, envy, wrath, sloth, avarice, gluttony, and lust. Each one, a single but essential step on the long and arduous journey up the mountain into paradise. »

The moonlight was a problem. Here, on the Western side of the mountain, Valériane was exposed. Anyone in the camp could look up at any time and see her silhouetted against the cliffs. But it was a necessary risk. This was the only path that was not guarded—a rugged climb over the mountaintop, scaling down a sheer face with only her own hands and feet. A rope would be spotted. It was too risky. Valériane was a skilled climber, but that was in the daylight. One poor hold, one shift of stone, and she would plummet. But she knew these cliffs well. It was her explorations of the area that had led to the discovery of the secret bay, her current destination. Some decades earlier, one of the archaeologists from this research site had found something in these hills. Valériane did not fully understand everything the researchers here said about the discovery, but their whispers of it were enough.

And she did understand one thing plainly:

within these cliffs was a hidden treasure.

That was worth the risk of scaling these cliffs in the late hours, after everyone ashore was asleep and the full moon was her only light source. It was worth everything, even her life. There was a cave in the belly of the cliffs which led to an interior chamber. It had been covered by a large basalt stone, about the width of a man's shoulders.

Valériane found the entrance of the cave, had climbed inside, and using one of the small cameras the research lab had given her, she had transmitted images back to her laptop. She was astonished by what she'd found. Treasure. Not gold, but many jewels. Items made of gems looking like diamonds that would fetch a great value, if they were sold. More wealth than Valériane had ever imagined in all her life, and all of it out of her reach, even as she stood inches from it.

Valériane used the camera to capture a sweeping view of the chamber. She could hear them over the little speakers in her ears. It went on for several minutes, as she stood in the 'treasure' vault, listening to them while studying the gems and walls of this place. When she decided to relay her search one night, the director of the lab told her to come back, and leave everything she'd found.

Valériane had not shown it to the other researchers but instead had stooped and quickly slipped it into her pocket, careful to keep the eye of the camera facing the other way. The following weeks orders were issued and researchers were busy organizing ways to get into the chamber, to use their ropes and equipment, and to have professional climbers do what Valériane had done with her bare hands.

No one knew she had one of the gems. One morning she found a small popular looking local eatery. The cafe owner counted on that business, Valériane knew, by the avid look of her round face with twinkling eyes. The young researcher wanted a place which had no name attached to it where she would not bump into anyone she knew officially. She found a rich looking man, sitting at a table looking at his mobile while sipping a chilled coffee. Something unusual for the locals to do. They mostly preferred a fizzy drink.

Valériane approached the gentleman and stood close, silent.

"Bonjour, it is me, I have something today," Valériane said, quietly. The guy looked around at the rest of the people in the cafe, but no one was paying attention to them. Or at least, no one seemed to be paying attention.

"You have something," the man said flatly. "Alright, let's see it." Valériane took a small box out of her pocket and placed it on the table, in front of the man.

The man looked at her face for a moment, then carefully opened the box revealing a cotton wad. He quickly uncovered it. He stared at the shining object, and gave Valériane a quizzical gaze, looking straight at her with his piercing cold grey eyes.

'What is it?!'

'I had it tested and it is a perfect diamond!'

'No ... it can't be! Where did you get this?' he asked drawing closer to take a better look.

Valériane knew that it was wise to keep such secrets to herself. Giving anything away meant giving it all away. This was crucial for her deal.

"It is a secret place. Only known to me. I can reach it, for now."

"Is it stolen? Did you find a treasure?!'

"I took it from a cave. I must climb a mountain to reach it. But there are other treasures there."

"How much treasure?" he asked sounding both nervous and exasperated.

Valériane knew she had to be careful. She wanted to entice this man, but giving him too much information would be dangerous.

"A few... far too many," Valériane said. "Many of them jewels. But there's something more exciting beyond these ..."

Again, the man studied her face, and Valériane wondered if he was believing her. Could he read her mind?'

"Can you bring me more?"

Valériane considered this. It would be difficult, but she believed she could return to the cave. It would mean another difficult climb. The moon was different now, as well. Less light. But she knew the cliff's face well.

"Yes," she said, finally. Are you interested? Will you buy this jewel and anything else I bring?"

The man reached his leather case and opened it revealing a thick stack of British pounds. It was more money than Valériane had ever seen in her life, at one go. The life of a researcher was arduous and not well remunerated neither for the long hours of work nor the discoveries. The funding money only paid for essentials for research to go on at the lab. She wanted more freedom, money she could spend on better equipment and leisure.

"Yes, I am in. Can you imagine what this means for you ...for us? Bring me everything you can, and I will pay you for it."

"But the gems...," Valériane said.

The man smiled at her and shook his head. He counted out some of the money he'd been holding, folded it, and put it in Valériane's open tote bag.

"Bring me everything you can," he stated decisively, getting up to go. Valériane also left the cafe and raced away to prepare, though there wasn't much preparation necessary. She grabbed her cloth sack, and a couple of other useful items. She carefully hid the money she'd been paid, wrapping it in a piece of upholstery cut from the seat of a wrecked automobile, at the village's edge.

She buried this deep in the soil, beneath a stone, and prayed over it, that it would be kept safe.

Several hours later, as the night came, Valériane once again scaled the cliff side, in the weak moonlight. She was less worried about anyone seeing her, this time, but more worried about a misstep. She held her nerve, however, and eventually climbed into the shaft.

Once she was a bit deeper in the shaft, she turned on the small flashlight that had been tucked into her pocket—something she'd stolen from one of the researchers. She tilted the light down and held it in between her teeth and made the descent, wedging her knees and elbows against the slanting stone and lowering herself a few inches at a time. It was slow progress, but once she reached the bottom, she moved rapidly. She would only be able to carry so much, so she would need to make this raid count. The gems were the priority, fortunately they were lightweight and small, easy to carry. She focused on the glimmering stones, illuminated and sparkling in the light of the flashlight. Using the blade of a knife, she pried at many of them, trying to remove them from the rocks as if they adhered like skin. They proved much more difficult to remove than she had anticipated. It was taking far too much time.

Valériane had started her climb at midnight, and it had taken a great deal of time to get to the cave. The longer she spent here, the closer it got to dawn. She could not risk climbing at a time when she could be spotted by anyone. Way too risky. She had almost decided to leave, to be content with the money she could fetch for this number of gems. As she passed the light around the space one last time, however, it landed on the largest of the gems—a reddish bluish one, the size of her palm. She peered closer. This one was set in a sheath which definitely looked like a fish skin. It gleamed like a rainbow and very inviting. She smiled and tucked it into the small sack she had slung over her shoulder. This would be her own piece.

Something she would keep to garner her buyer to hike the price he was offering. She had decided this was enough, and was about to make the climb out when she noticed a door behind a basalt boulder. It was tucked away, behind a bend in the stone cavern, and she'd only caught a glimpse of its outer edge as her flashlight beam passed over the space. It reflected back at her in a golden hue. What was that?!, she crawled her way towards the door. Maybe it was a vault of some kind? It might have other treasures; her greed was now taking over her mind! Perhaps a pirate's hidden trove? She wouldn't be surprised as the island was full of the legends of these notorious figures who were believed to have hidden their bounty somewhere. Many have devoted their lives into searching for them.

The door was covered in lichen and barnacles. She took out her knife and scratched some, what was beneath was shiny. Brass ... gold? It rose high above her head. It was covered with strange symbols she had found everywhere in the cavern. A Celtic style knot-work of etchings twisted up and around the door's edge. In the centre of the door, surrounded by vines of angular symbols, was a face. It was smooth, and frightening. Like the face of a sea monster. Valériane had seen similar faces, carved into stone and wood, recovered from the dig site by the researchers. But this was the first time she'd seen it cast in brass or gold. She reached out, and put her hand on it, running her fingers over its features. The face moved under her hand, sinking into the surface of the door, and ... Its eyes and mouth opened. Valériane screamed, jerking her hand swiftly away and scurrying back into the main chamber. She clambered up and over the black basalt rocks, quickly moving to the exit. She scrambled up into it and climbed as quickly as she dared, praying for protection as she ascended. When she reached the surface, the moon had dipped below the distant ridge line, and the light was scant. She picked her way up the cliff face, reaching for handholds out of memory and hope. She was moving too fast, and she knew it. But her fear was giving her limbs increased strength, and she was keenly aware of every crack and crevice on the cliff's facade.

Soon she crested the top, and she ran, making speed down the hillside. She did not stop until she was back in the village.

The next morning, she found the man, and after some explanation that this was all she could find, she made the sale. It was indeed a great sum of money. It would get her all she wished for, for her lab and much more. Before she could leave, the man grabbed her arm, squeezing hard. "Tell me where you found these?" he asked. "Where is this treasure?" Afraid, Valériane told him everything she knew. She told him of the climb, and of the vault of treasure, though he had wanted to keep it secret. She described the gems.

"There is a guardian in the vault," she said, her voice going quiet. "A creature guarding it.”

“Creature?” the man asked. Valériane told him about the face in the door. The man listened, then let her go.

She hastily left the man sitting at a table in the café. He watched her go. When Valériane had disappeared into the crowd at the junction where it joined the main road to the city centre, the man looked again at one of the shiny objects Valériane had left him, running his fingers around its engraved edges. He recognized the symbols. He knew what this was. He closed the sack again, and took out his mobile, tapping a number he had dialled many times. “I have found it,” the man said. “How soon can you get here?”

*

"What's most exciting to archaeologists,

especially in anthropology and the study of human culture, is usually pretty boring to everyone else. It's a lot of scraping and dusting, really."

Jonas recorded his recent research and findings. Since his strange encounter on the beach, he had devoted hours and days into trying to understand what had happened to him. He wrote to a few of his contemporaries around the world with resounding assumptions and probable answers. But no one could really point out anything beyond a mythical figure of a mermaid who sang to sailors to their death. Until he read some research from a South Indian anthropologist. It was riveting how much everything made sense. He had yet to convince his scientific fraternity.

He watched again a piece of video he was sent. The image on screen changed and morphed, as if a camera were pulling back to reveal a rotating globe. The continents were recognizable, and floating above all of them, like 3D projections emitted from the ground, were glowing images of archaeological sites, of artefacts, ancient temples, statues, and other objects. The effect was impressive, as if the entire world were alive with the discovery of history and ancient cultures.

"All around the world, from cultures as disparate and separate from each other as time and terrain can make them, we keep running into something remarkable. From cultures that should have nothing in common, we find commonality."

Several of the images floating above the virtual terrain moved to the centre of the screen, aligning with each other. Each image portrayed a repetitive stack of stones—

vertical pillars with a large, horizontal stone as a roof. "You probably recognize the image in the middle: Stonehenge, located in Wiltshire, England. Perhaps the most famous primitive stone structure to survive to modern day, and one that we most commonly associate with early Indo-European culture. The voice over continued:

"At a period in history when none of the humans who lived in these regions had the means or technology to travel the globe, they somehow shared commonalities. Not just structures, not just the impulse to make a mark on one's environment. There are symbols—the rudiments of language—that appear across history and cultures, seemingly, completely disconnected from each other."

Another image replaced the hands from Lascaux caves to a swastika, this time of a single symbol that grew to fill the screen.

"Perhaps the most recognizable symbol of the Nazi party, and one we have come to associate with hate and horror on an unimaginable scale. The swastika morphed into a variety of presentations, from simple carvings and sculptures to ornate medallions, from bits of broken clay pottery to gold-laden temple walls. Some appeared in ancient artwork, with motifs ranging from seahorses to eagles.

Native American artwork appeared alongside a golden brooch from India. The swastika pops up throughout history. Nazi Germany, of course, put to its most infamous use. It also appears in Russia, no surprise. But perhaps most surprisingly to appear significantly earlier in North American culture, among artwork from early Navajo tribes. On baskets and blankets, each bearing the Swastika, "predate European settlement of the Americas by hundreds of years. In fact, this symbol is known as the 'whirling logs,' among the Navajo, and it's tied to the story of a great hero. The swastika, or whirling log, is a symbol of great wisdom, given by the gods.

Further back, we find the symbol in Iraq, Armenia, Korea, and among what we think of as the primitive cultures. The Anglo Saxons. The Thracians. Even in some neolithic artwork. The Swastika led to another grid of images, this time of gods from various pantheons, including an image of Jesus. The voice over continued: "Here we see Osiris, Marduk, Adonis, Tammuz, Aliyan Baal, Viracocha, and of course, Jesus Christ. Each of these represents the concept of the 'Dying-and-Rising deity.' But there's a more profound mystery here. In every recorded culture, in every pantheon, there exists a god who died and was resurrected.

From the Sumerians and Babylonians, the Greeks and Romans, the Celtic Druids and even the Mayans and Aztecs, they each have their god of resurrection." "And there are other commonalities in these pantheons. Gods who not only served the same purpose—a god of harvests, and god of rains, a god of sexuality—but who very often shared histories. Osiris shares a similar origin story with Moses, for example. As similar to that of Lord Krishna. Krishna's father Vasudeva was carrying the new-born Krishna to safety while crossing Yamuna river and asked the latter to make a way for him to cross the river, by creating a passage. Both had family members who feared for their safety and constructed floating vessels to send them down the Nile or Yamuna. Both are found and raised by foster parents. The order of these events and the ages of the heroes may differ slightly, but the details are all there."

"In anthropology, we refer to this as 'comparative mythology.' We are looking at these great cultures, at these pantheons and myths, to find the commonality. We want to know why these stories appear, again and again, even in cultures that have never been in contact with each other. And we want to solve the mystery of origin, for the various cultures worldwide. Every ancient culture has a mythology of gods and heroes. The biggest question we ask, when studying all of these, is where did they go? Were these myths based on actual, living beings? And if so, what happened to the gods, and why did they become extinct?"

On the immense screen, the globe reappeared, rotating slowly, with images rising from one horizon and disappearing over the next. The Earth was filling up with the images of archaeological dig sites and ancient artefacts.

"So many cultures. And every day, as we dig deeper into our past, we're discovering more. There is no doubt as to the similarities between each, but the thing that unites them remains a mystery. Where did they come from? How is it possible that they share so many similarities? There are these artefacts, for sure, but there are also shared mythologies. Similarities in oral traditions, in superstitions, in religious observations. Every major culture has a flood myth, for example. There are also myths of powerful prophets, deaths and resurrections, gods walking among men. Over and over,

throughout history, we've discovered and rediscovered the hints of a civilization that remains shrouded and hidden. Somehow, in some way, a culture that unites all of humanity came and went, and we barely have any hint of it."

"But that's changing. Every day, in disparate parts of the world, we're finding the traces of that extinct civilization. We are writing the history that was lost, with each new discovery. Recent geological discovery of zirconium in Mauritius led to the speculation that it could not have originated from the volcanic spew but rather a resurfacing of elements that predates the existence of the island itself. Out of her 9 million years, the granite and basalt are legit but not a zirconium. That requires some solid geological workings of billions of years. It spells out that this can

originate from a continental shelf older than we see visible today around Mauritius.'

'An unusual civilization and, although very different from modern times, a very advanced society even by today's standards existed in an area which today makes one of the largest oceans in the world. Many called it Lemuria, the continent probably had another name that is now forgotten.

The word "Lemuria" came to be associated with this part of the world when scientists in the mid-1800's found a species of monkeys known as lemurs, which resembled a cross between a monkey and a squirrel. Lemurs have a human-looking face, and it was once believed that they were part of the evolutionary line for the human race. They are not. However, the lemurs are still prevalent on the island of

Madagascar off the coast of Africa as well as on the African mainland, in India and Indonesia. Scientists speculated that, in order to have the lemurs inhabiting all these varied, unconnected areas, there once must have been a land bridge for them to traverse.

In 1870, an English zoologist, Philip L. Sclater, gave the submerged lands of the Indian Ocean the name "Lemuria" in honour of the lemurs. Although no one ever formally declared "Lemuria" as the official name for this submerged area. Continued usage over time made the name synonymous with this lost landmass and the civilization who resided there.

In the 1930's, a retired British colonel, James Churchward, gave the name Mû to the lost land mass in the pacific which in reality should have been the Indian Ocean.

An inventor and engineer, Churchward spent the latter part of his life trying to prove Mû's existence. He claimed to have found the name "Mû" on ancient tablets hidden in a monastery where he resided for a short time while he was stationed in India. No one else has ever seen these tablets, so his word that these ancient lands were known as Mû is all that is available. Although the zoologist Sclater probably meant to use the term Lemuria for just the sunken land in the Indian Ocean, the name came to be associated with the lost continent in the Pacific Ocean as well.

All that is certain is that both the areas in the Pacific Ocean and those in the Indian Ocean were once one large, connected land mass. That would make Lemuria a predecessor of not only the Polynesian Islands but also Japan, Australia, New

Zealand, the Indonesian Islands, India, Tibet, Ceylon, and Madagascar. For the purposes of this book, popular usage will be honoured, and the name Lemuria will refer to the lost lands in both the Pacific and Indian Oceans. One might ask if there is no scientific proof that Lemuria ever really existed, then where can information concerning this civilization be found. References to Lemuria and its people for the most part reside in material from paranormal sources.

Since not all of these sources are completely reliable, each source should be evaluated as to whether or not the information can be authenticated. One way to verify paranormal information is to cross check the data with either historical or other reliable paranormal sources. When more than one of these sources agree on a certain *point, the information receives a higher rate of validity and presents a greater possibility of being true. The following sections in this chapter will examine several of the more prominent paranormal sources who have contributed the larger body of information regarding the ancient civilization of Lemuria.*

It was reported that the Lemurians belonged to the "third root race." A root race is a term that designates the large periods of time marking the various stages in human evolution. According to the Theosophists, there will be seven root races, each composed of seven sub races. Modern man belongs to the fifth root race, and Blavatsky claimed that the sixth root race will evolve from the present Homo sapiens, returning to live in Lemuria.

The Lemurians are described in Blavatsky's

book as gigantic, apelike creatures with no brains. It was claimed that some Lemurians had four arms and some had an eye on the back of their head. It was this "eye" that gave them their psychic vision. Lemurians communicate telepathically and use no other language at all. While some of them made their homes in caves, others dug huge holes in the ground to use as homes.

Rejected by the scientific community in his lifetime, the ideas of the previously mentioned James Churchward are making a comeback today. Several journalists who reported on the underwater discoveries of ancient structures near Japan in 1995 included Churchward's name as a major source of information regarding these ancient sites now buried under the sea. A few even went so far as to link Mu to the underwater city that covers nearly 311 miles near Okinawa and beyond the island of Yonaguni. Although the discovery put Lemuria in the forefront again, a study of Lemurian life-style shows that this civilization didn't erect large structures. Therefore, these recently discovered sizable man-made platforms and stone archways found underwater near Japan along with those found near Cuba and the island of Bimini are all probably remnants of Atlantean construction. Churchward wrote five books on Lemuria or Mu and had extensive notes for a sixth one that was eventually published in 1997, long after his death. These book titles include 'The Lost Continent of Mu', Motherland of Man, The Children of Mu, 'The Sacred Symbols of Mu', and 'Cosmic Forces of Mu'.

Churchward used the name Mu exclusively in his writings and advocated that the lost *continent of Mu now forms the ocean floor for the Pacific Ocean. He offered proof of Mu's existence in various ways, but mostly through symbols found on pottery, recovered walls and pillars of temple decorations found in Mexico, buried tablets also found in Mexico, and stone markers or rock formations in the American Southwest. His proof even included linking the symbols used in the ancient alphabets of such countries as Greece and India with the symbols associated with Mu. Although his information intrigued the general public and armchair anthropologists, by the time Churchward published his books on Mu, he had antagonized too many important people in the influential social strata. This rift may be a key contributing factor to the ridicule his work on Mu met on the scientific front. The major cause of this antagonism was the lawsuit victories Churchward and his long-time friend and patent attorney, Percy Tate Griffith, won against Carnegie Steel in 1910 and Bethlehem Steel in 1915. Churchward, an engineer, had invented a fine steel known in the industry as NCV Steel that was lightweight yet strong enough to be used in the construction of warships.*

Other steel companies had infringed on his patent and were already selling it to the American government. Churchward was blackballed out of the steel industry after his court victories, forcing him and Griffith to sell the invention to a small steel company. However, the court victories gave Churchward the money he needed to pursue his first love, namely finding proof of the existence of Mu.

Another contributing factor to the mistrust of Churchward's information on Mu, by the experts, was their inability to prove the source of his claims of where he learned the symbols of Mu. According to Churchward, he studied these symbols from ancient Naacal (displaced people from the lost continent of Lemuria) tablets and was taught their translations by his hosts during his stay in a monastery while stationed in India with the British army.

Yet, when others returned to this same monastery to authenticate the existence of these tablets, the monks would not admit them and denied any existence of these tablets. With this turn of events, Churchward's credibility was lost until modern times. It was adventurer David Hatcher Childress, author of Lost Cities of Ancient Lemuria and the Pacific, who pointed out that the Rosicrucian Order of San Jose, California, claims to have access to a number of secret libraries hidden all over Tibet. If that is the case, says Childress, then Churchward's secret Mu tablets are not so unbelievable, especially in light of the additional discovery that monks in India are highly selective about who are actually admitted to their monasteries. In other words, while Churchward had gained the monks' trust, those researchers that followed asking to see the same tablets were denied access because the monks decided they would not be admitted for one reason or another. Although there is information in the Churchward books that cannot be authenticated or verified, new discoveries and technology have solidified some of his theories and advanced his credibility.

In almost any mention of Lemuria today, Churchward is referenced and oftentimes considered an important source on the lost continent of the Pacific even though he is still not fully sanctioned by the scientific community.

There continues to be a variety of sources contributing information about Lemuria. On the academic front, the science of DNA may eventually replace archaeological digs to prove the existence of past civilizations. For instance, Greg and Laura Little in their book Ancient South America point to research that provides evidence through the study of DNA that the people of the Pacific originated from a group of islands in the southwestern portion of the Pacific known as Melanesia and nearby Indonesia. Moreover, the Littles wrote that because the people of the South Pacific inhabited these islands for so long, it is estimated by the experts that their place of origin is their present location. Although no one has come forth to admit that this research based on DNA may someday be a part of the proof that a Lemurian civilization once existed there, these possibilities are now at least under discussion.

All matters of science on Lemuria are based on the translations of two sets of ancient tablets.

Naacal tablets which were discovered in India many years ago, and a large collection of stone tablets, over 2500, recently discovered by William Niven in Mexico. Both sets have the same origin; for both sets are extracts from the Sacred Inspired Writings of Mu. The Naacal tablets are written with the Naga symbols and characters—and, legend says, were written in the Motherland and first brought to Burma and then to India. Their extreme age is attested to by the fact that history says the Naacals left Burma more than 15,000 years ago. Where the Mexican tablets were written is problematical. They are mostly written in the northern or Uighur symbols and characters. What actual writing there is on both sets is in the alphabet of Mu, the Motherland. Whether they were written in Mexico or in the Motherland and brought to Mexico is not certain. They are, however, over 12,000 years old as shown by some of the tablets.

The Garden of Eden may not be in Asia but on a now sunken continent in the Pacific Ocean. The Biblical story of creation—the epic of the seven days and the seven nights—came first not from the peoples of the Nile or of the Euphrates Valley but from this now submerged continent. Mu—the Motherland of Man. These assertions can be proved by the complex records discovered upon long-forgotten sacred tablets in India, together with records from other countries. They tell of this strange country of 64,000,000 inhabitants, who, 50,000 years ago, had developed a civilization superior in many respects to our own. They described, among other things, the creation of man in the mysterious land of Mu. By comparing this writing with records of other ancient civilizations, as revealed in written documents, prehistoric ruins and geological phenomena, it was found that all these centres of civilization had drawn their culture from a common source—Mu. We may, therefore, be sure that the Biblical story of the creation as we know it today may have evolved from the impressive account gathered from those ancient tablets which relate the history of Mu— history 500 centuries old.'

The audience was silent. Everyone was dazed by such revelations. It was a lot to take in. Jonas caught his breath and drank some sparkling water. He was not sure how the audience would react. The silence was a bit daunting. It took courage to have exposed his theories. He still had a quiver by his chin which he tried taming by drinking some water and scanning faces. No reaction. Had he gone too far? Right now, all he wanted to do was make a quick exit and breathe some fresh air.

Gondwana and Meru

'It had the river Paktuli at the north and the river Kumari at the south were the physical state lines. Equally, the rivers had the source in the Meru Ghats which had partitioned the north and south land mass. Having little awareness of Meru Mountain, the literary translators had considered the

Himalayas by mistake as the Meru Ghats, which has been proved false. For, the Himalayan Mountain had never existed during the total epoch Gondwana and the whole of north India was identified as the area where the sea water was running in between.

The word 'Mel Uru' is the word shrunk into 'Meru' which had been called as Su-Meru. 'Su' means 'Yezhu' (seven in English) which represents the seven mountains.

The Submerged 'Kumari Continent' Thamizh people were fond of the number Yezhu (Seven). Yezhu kadal (seven seas, which also implies the meaning overseas), Yezhu Malai (Seven mountains, also meaning beyond the lands), Yezhu Aruhal (Seven Rivers), Yezhu Ulaham (Seven worlds) are all up to date usage. The popular name of people 'Venkada Malai'

(Venkada Mountains) is branded as 'Yezhumalai'. The civilized world of Kumari Continent is found more in world literature than in Thamizh literary works- since they were torn down.

Most of the historical events found in Thamizh literature are tedious to read and hang about afar from credence. Containing quotations of various people from an assortment of ages and regions, they have to be brought to the surface by reading and delving into world literature. Pavanar the greatest literary intellectual of Thamizh, turned out a lot of corroborations based on the theory 'Kumari Continent', wherein he was so self-assured of.

Scholars of the world and even Thamizh Nadu scoffed at his works and put him under derision telling that he had been blowing his own trumpet and the Thamizh people and their terrain. Most of them believed that there existed no 'Kumari Continent'

Thamizh scholars who have 'Anti-Thamizh Thought' and entrust to memory that the fore said people who speak against Tamil will perish with their ideas, knowing the truth of the Tamil origin and Kumari Continent.

The Indian government has endowed a large sum of money on the archaeological research in the Indian Ocean where lord Krishna's Duvaraha or Dwarka, the birthplace lies beneath.

Some of the Thamizh writers, mostly in the later part of the 19th century and the early part of the 20th century confused the Kumari Continent with the so-called Lemurian Continent in their writings as their own discovery.

The lost Lemuria Continent was a scientific fiction and it was proven false once and for all. The Lemurian Continent never existed nor was it ever submerged.'

Jonas was glad he managed to finish his expansive presentation, but he was also exhausted. The excitement, the tension, the anxiety that came from going through the research papers led him to an exciting idea. But for now, a cold beer would go down well.

He finished packing and headed to his little haven. The day had been long. He badly needed a cool drink and some rest.

10

Mû

"Mû was politically united, but it wasn't at peace. Spiritually, its citizens were not at all united. Black vines crawled across the ground and wrapped around stone coral, and strange vegetation flourished that wouldn't grow anywhere else. The air in this dome was as thick as the water outside and almost unbreathable.

When the priestess was drowned alongside the whole kingdom, the continent was submerged for 3 billions of years. Until apes evolved, after the later continents drifted apart. They walked upright, moved to the north and muted into light skinned humans. Led by their hunter-gathering instinct they moved across the continents again, created races, then nations, then boundaries, fought each other, made peace again and advanced into mechanical, technological led societies.

Until one day, crept a creature as lithe as air, as transparent as water from the sea to the shore. Everything it touched camouflaged itself into its image. Every cell was a tiny diamond. It was born of the tears of the priestess when she was drowned by her lover, Shrava. She vowed she would come back and seek revenge for each and every life that perished on Mû.

Billions of years later, when the world changed, life regained its consciousness from the ancient lost continent. The creatures came to the outside world from the depths of the ocean. Each night, they left the water to explore the shore. They shine like little jewels among the rocks. In the thick of the night, only the stars rivalled their brilliance.

It was on such a lone dark night, that Valériane took a stroll to the beach. She sat for a long time on the large flat black basalt pillow lavas soaking in the beauty of the sea and the sky. She kept still for a long time, as if trying to merge herself into the vastness of the sky above her, when she saw a shining object flick. She squinted to adjust her sight into the darkness. It moved again, this time precisely into a step. It wasn't a hop. Then it grew in height. From a tiny shiny fleck, it assumed the height of a human.

Valériane felt she wasn't breathing anymore, she kept as still as humanely possible. The creature shone in the darkness like a brightly lit glowing Christmas tree. It advanced towards the rocks and suddenly disappeared. Valériane felt she could breathe again. She gasped, looked slowly around her and waited. After a quarter of an hour, she got up, and tread her steps back to her car. She was sure the creature was somewhere around but where? She started the car and drove slowly away.

The next morning, she laid awake in her bed thinking what she saw. The day went by slowly as Valériane was bent into going back to the spot to try to see again what that thing was; patience was a virtue which she had loads.

With nightfall, she made her way again to the spot and waited. Waited. Till when it was about half past midnight, she saw a faint glow in the water. And it emerged. As shiny as the previous night. This time Valériane held her breath, but looked very attentively. The thing didn't seem to notice her. Or pretended not to? It made its way to the rocks again and this time Valériane saw the morphing or rather an unknown form of camouflaging.

The young woman's heart was racing and thumped loudly in her ears. She wished she could quieten it. What was happening was so surreal as if she was seeing live one of her comics she read when she was young. The cloudy sky blocked even the faintest light from the stars and other celestial objects. The sea was tranquil, and a soft, cool breeze gently ruffled her hair. She waited again for some time, then left.

The next morning, she went back to the exact spot where the 'thing' disappeared. She scrutinized the spot in all the nooks and crannies. Walked in the shallows, when suddenly a tiny flash caught her eye. The sun's rays were directly shining something like fool's gold in a tiny rockpool. She bent down and gently picked the object. It was tiny like a grey mullet's scale but was solid like a gem. It shone like a diamond. She took out her handkerchief and wrapped the gem-like scale in it.

Valériane was old school, she always carried a handkerchief with her. As a child, she would douse it with lavender Bien-Être cologne and smell it the whole day in class. She loved the fresh scent and it provided a barrier to the smell of sweat her classmates carried after playing in the sun.

Valériane followed her investigation about the strange gem-like scale she recovered. She tried testing it with several solutions in her lab. No results. She couldn't classify it as a specific chemical or mineral. Nothing in the periodic table, it seemed like a new compound. She decided to take it to a jeweller to get an artisan's view on it. What she found would stun her. The jeweller was one of Rose Hill's best known in town. He took it to his back-door room to examine the piece in detail. There sat his small machine which never failed to authenticate a fake.

He had been looking closely at the gem-like scale with his magnifying jeweller's viewfinder. He was speculating for only one possibility. He had been given a request by this beautiful and charming young white woman who insisted he checked this object with all urgency. He couldn't say no, despite his heavy backlog of work.

When he placed the object in the grip of the arm in the machine, he felt it was warm. Something unlike a gemstone. He held it for a moment and felt as if it was pulsating. Unsettled, he proceeded with the ultimate test. The machine soon started hissing in a high pitch. He stopped the machine, un lodged the object carefully, and walked out the back door to the front side of his shop. Valériane was sitting waiting, and when she saw him appearing, she stood up at once.

'Alors ?'

'*Madame c'est un diamant !*'

'*Quoi?! Oh Mon Dieu!*' Valériane almost choked in shock. The jeweller looked at her quite puzzled. He couldn't make out what the object was, it didn't look crafted. It didn't look as if it was a piece of adornment either. What was it?

'What is it? Where did you find it?'

'Oh, I don't even know ... I found it

somewhere. I need to know what it is... how much do I owe you?'

'*Rien* - it is OK, but please can you tell me what it is when you find out?'

His jeweller's curiosity was piqued and he felt it was a strange piece by the way it pulsated in his hand. He had never felt anything like that in his life. As if it was a living thing.

As Valériane hastily thanked him with effusion, she strode to the door, but the jeweller hailed her.

'*Madame*, I forgot to tell you ...'

'What?!' Valériane retreated and stepped back to the counter. The jeweller looked intensively at her and said 'no real gem is ever warm, yet this one is, and it has a pulse'

Valériane took it with wide eyes and couldn't find a reply.

She thanked him again and left.

11

Shi

Shi, a senior Valli of the rank of high commander of Mû, was preparing for yet another battle. She was the daughter of a Kalapathi of the imperial coastal fleet. Her father had inspired her to join the naval army around three years ago, much against the wishes of her mother.

Tall and dusky with an athletic build, she was blessed with a sharp intellect and had a penchant for martial arts. The long hours she spent in practicing the ancient martial art of Shila-shashtra, had made her an exceptional warrior. She was proficient in a variety of close combat weapons and unarmed techniques. Her long wavy black hair was neatly tied into a tight bun behind her neck, with a few poison-tipped darts always pinned into it. She was widely recognized for her supreme skills in precision archery, high-speed dart throwing, and other close combat techniques. She was inducted into the squad just before they set out on the ambitious overseas military expedition of the Imperial Mû naval army. Her sharp features, high cheekbones and large, fish-shaped eyes, gave her a very elegant yet bewitchingly seductive appearance.

Every time Shrava saw her, he was reminded of someone from his past, with whom he had an emotional relationship. Over the past year out at sea, he had quickly developed a special fondness for Shi, though he never openly displayed it. She however, did not attempt to conceal her emotions for him and preferred to spend most of her free time in his company. She knew very well that he would never object to that. She also knew that he too secretly looked forward to the time they spent with each other every day. He now watched her as she did a quick inspection of the team's specialized equipment, and made final preparations to slip into the dark waters below.

The rest of the team followed her into the gloomy depths, in quick succession. They immediately began their long swim below the waves towards the ships anchored just outside the port. Their camouflaged outfits helped them to remain undetected by the enemy. They were invisible to the sword-wielding guards pacing along the decks of the ships. The sentries on lookout platforms, high up on the main masts of the enemy ships were oblivious to the swiftly approaching commandos.

As the special team slipped through the shadowy depths of the ocean, the forwards kept a watchful eye on the enemy. They anxiously watched the surface of the waters around the ships for tell-tale signs of their compatriots. In less than fifteen minutes, they noticed ripples just below the enemy ships. Eight black silhouetted heads broke through the surface of the water, away from the line of sight of the sentries above. They promptly re-grouped once more before the final assault. The commandos sent up a silent prayer to Lord Murugan, before they split up again, gliding like invisible ghosts below the water. Victory was theirs.

Shi was elevated to the legion of warrior supreme priestess. She spent more days being protected and surrounded by guards rather than serving in far-away conquests. Shrava and herself got close after she had had a few more lovers. Their idyll became the talk of the kingdom. For some reason, Shrava never talked about making their love 'official'. He met her at the peak of the night and would depart before the break of dawn. Shi felt there was something the young man was after but couldn't put her finger on it. Sometimes he would be passionately amorous and at other times seemed cold and calculating.

Shi was invested as the head priestess by the king, and was given the star and key of the main gates to the oceans. Which meant she held the life of all the kingdom in her hands. A responsibility she was entrusted with because of her great integrity and strength. Shrava admired these qualities of the young woman. However, the cloud between them persisted. Until it would prove fatal.

She was being groomed to become one of the most enlightened women in Mû, but it did not appear as though she was at all interested in following her designated path. She was a Kumari. Even she did not understand why she could not embrace her future. She just couldn't get into it, as they say. Many hopes rested with her, but unknowingly, she sensed that Mû had lowered its vibration; therefore, she had to create a new definition of Mûian spirituality for herself. The joy and bliss she experienced, just by being whom she felt she was meant to be, came from deep within her heart. The concept of a linear future reaches into the past with delicate fingers, trying gently and gracefully to mould and shape it into a better present; but how is one to know which changes will be better and which will not? Mû was not a perfect place, by any means, there were those who cared about what was best for all and there were those who thought only of themselves.

Then there are the heroes, without which society would never be lifted higher, but would continue down an incline towards desolation. Through grace, heroes exist, not ever relinquishing their spirit to move forward. Shi's parents nurtured her the best way they knew how, but their efforts to groom her for the Keepership role of her destiny seemed fruitless.

Unbeknownst to them, their efforts were not in vain, but it would be a long time before they saw the Keeper of the Principles of Divine Grace emerge.

A Kumari couldn't fail her people. Her fate was sealed into safeguarding all those around her.

They did not understand that part of her true purpose was to live in the everyday world, so she could integrate the protective energy necessary to shield her from the gradual lowering of the vibration of the Golden Age of Mû, as Lord Murugan had intended Himself.

She was the chosen one.

Not many people saw the slow decline, as there were only a few individuals who had become tainted by human frailty, a trait that is taken for granted in the modern world. Those fallen few affected the whole and without anyone knowing, the process had begun. Greed, lust for power, and deceit did not exist in the Golden Age of Mû, although they had heard of such things in ancient civilizations that had fallen. To most, it was a paradise, but paradise is a relative term.

*

'What we know of the Earth was very much as it is today in many ways, but there were also considerable differences. Areas that are currently tropical were temperate and other places that are now deserts were lush gardens. However, in essentials, things were much as they have always been when humans are involved. Babies were born, people loved and lost and life continued from day to day, the particulars of which, in one of the most advanced cultures the Earth has seen, had the obvious characteristics of such a world. For practical purposes, this story will be told in linear terms, even though the time frame of both worlds is completely different from

each other. You will be going from an undeviating time dimension to a multi-dimensional one. This is a story though, not a lesson in Quantum Physics; therefore, the rules and guidelines of the Third Dimensional structural reality will be observed.

It is said that people lived much longer in those days, but it is all relative. Time did not pass at the same rate there as it does here, for time is a product of consciousness, a system of lining up events that have occurred for purposes of reference. Atlantis had several different races of people, as does the Earth today. In similar fashion, humans in this dimension and those in Atlantis were seeded on the planet by inhabitants of different Star Systems, which had varied characteristics and abilities. The technology of the parent Star

Systems was brought to Earth and deployed, as the new planet was formed, so that the recently seeded beings could flourish, as was hoped and expected. The aliens, as we refer to them, came from Pleiades, Sirius, and Arcturus. They remained on Earth for eons, assisting in the evolutionary process of humanity, by tweaking the human DNA, until they were satisfied with the outcome. Many forms of humans evolved and became extinct over the ages until the hybrid species, the one that inhabits the Earth today, remained. All this was done while observing Divine Laws, so that only that which was decreed by the Creator was allowed to flourish, ensuring that humanity was able to continue living reasonably on Earth. When Divine Laws are not observed, the result is suffering, as may be witnessed on a daily basis. However, this does not imply failure, for it is all part of a plan by which people can realize many possibilities, as they continue to experience free will. Ancient culture and wisdom, which in modern times, have been labelled as fable or mythology, are actually an account of earlier periods of history on Earth. Perhaps one day historians will acknowledge Atlantis, Lemuria and other civilizations as our ancestral lands. They will begin to understand that the reason so many people living today is drawn to learning about these so-called myths is that they have recollections of other lives, which have remained in their cellular memory.'

Jonas finished his presentation and switched off the projector, lending the floor to question time.

Many journalists had come to attend after he had given a brief interview in the local dailies about a probable lost continent on which the island of Mauritius sat.

The tea break allowed many to crowd around Jonas and bombard him with questions. He had a theory and half of it with some evidence, the rest was pure speculation.

And speculation, he knew, never went down very well with the media. His motivation was also the fact of what he saw and experienced on the beach and a recent unsolved murder. The beach was proving to be an important part of the whole mesh of events. He had also recently stumbled upon the research of a geological anthropologist who reckoned the island had diamonds around its waters.

Jonas got himself ready for the latter part of his presentation. He noticed a white man watching him intensely. He didn't approach him during the break. He looked like a rich man, well dressed in a two-piece khaki linen trousers and blazer, wore dark glasses and held a small cane. Jonas thought he might come and talk to him after his last speech. Or not. There are some people who just like to listen and leave.

So, Jonas made his way to the front of the room, lights went dim, and he started:

'To live completely alone, in the midst of throngs of people, is an amazing experience. In this unknown continent, time passed as it most assuredly does in the present. Much like floating on a cloud, above the hard ground of life, the total freedom and perfection of existence had reached its fruition.'

Cruel ocean tides will churn and twist,
Birthing forth three glittering Jewels,

Poseidon himself can't stop their fate,

For one day, they will rule.

Anger festers in the heart,

Determination in their heads,

The laws say they must earn their place,

And feed the seas with death.

Jean Baptiste, Virginie, Mohan and many more;

Released from the world of men,

Sink a ship, fulfil your rite,

Be born again,

swimming till the end of time.

Jonas woke up from his vivid dream and tried recalling the details. He couldn't make any sense to them, but rather swept all of it behind his mind and got out of the bed to face the day. There was a neat envelope waiting for him at the lobby. The tall dark Hindu girl flashed her bright white smile to

him while handing the envelope to Jonas.
He sat by the opulent lobby sofas and lavish
art works, wondering what message it
contained. It was a simple short sentence
scribbled in a tiny cursive handwriting.

« Meet me here in the lobby.

Tomorrow at 3:00 p.m. »

Fabio Grignon

12

Michel Ducasse

The square-built, green-tiled house stared stonily at him as he swung the car into the drive. The tall bushes that lined the path made no sound to him as he walked past: there was no breeze to rustle through the thick branches, of the overgrown *badamier* (African almond) and mango trees. Inside the house it was silent too.

There had been a period, after Valériane had died, when Michel Ducasse had thought that peace would never return to the house.

There was the coming and going of police photographers, the fingerprint experts, the constables and the inspectors. There were the local reporters. There were the morbid sightseers and more inquisitive ghouls who came up to the house to peer in at the windows and gabble at the panes. It had been a wearing time, a difficult time, particularly since his nerves had been frayed by the insistent questioning as to his whereabouts, his relationship with his

wife, her address when she had left him, her friends, her enemies, — and his.

Michel Ducasse stayed with his wife from time to time when she was embarked on a long research on the island. She kept mum about it most times and revealed very little when Michel queried. They had come to an agreement that each one will pursue what they want and keep their freedom.

Michel has had a few flings in Paris to keep out the loneliness he felt sometimes. He wasn't aware how much he was missed by his wife. She always avoided the topic. He knew she was onto something big by her excitement over the phone and promised she would tell him soon. That was strange. As Valériane never promised anything to him. She also said that he would feel proud of her for her discovery. Again, very strange, for she also never expected him to be proud of her work. They lived in their parallel worlds without any complaints.

So, Michel's world came to a crash when he was contacted by the French Embassy in Mauritius, to inform him about the disappearance of Valériane. A couple of days ago he received a text message to summon him to the island, and that they believe that they discovered a body which matched the

DNA of Valériane. His world stopped making any sense to him. He was then informed that it had turned into a murder investigation and he was summoned to the island. Murder?! Valeriane? Who could possibly have killed his wife? She was content in her own world and never made any friends or foes. Best of all, she was self-effaced. A murder needs a motive. Michel had been drilling into all his memories of his wife, he couldn't find anything plausible that could lead to a murder motive.

He had arrived at the house after a very restless journey, meeting the officials and learning about their recent findings. The body of Valériane was in a terrible state. Further investigation from the coroner also suggested the woman was pregnant! That was a punch in his stomach. Knowing that Valériane had a lover was one but the utter shock was of her pregnancy. The couple had battled to have a child and the woman never felt she really wanted one. That was surely a revelation.

Valériane and Michel had wanted to live half the year on the island after they had visited it during one of their visits. Valériane wanted a house away from the town, in the wilder corners in the north. When they found this house, she was overjoyed and put her bags down. This had become their haven ever since, until distance between them crept into their relationship. Without either of them knowing how and why.

The kitchen door faced him and Michel hesitated. He should have something to eat: his lunch had been non-existent, with the morning inquest unsettling him. But right now, he needed a drink. He turned into the sitting-room, and walked across to the cocktail cabinet. It was a piece of tasteless affectation that Valériane had chosen for the offense it would give to Michel.

There was also the ridiculous little chiming clock, all gilt and cheap looking. With a liberal hand Michel poured himself a whisky. He took a stiff gulp from the glass, then sat down with his back to the French windows that overlooked the long narrow lawn at the back of the house, flanked by the enormous rose-bed that had been planted before they moved into the house.

Last summer the roses had bloomed in magnificence. Recent rain had dulled them this year and since Valériane's death the gardener had not come and the weeds had thickened around the soggy base of the rose bushes.

Since Valériane's death . . . It was perhaps

not strange that he should now measure everything by that event. It was hardly surprising that he should think of her as she was before. He couldn't recognise her delicate features, her tiny nose, her gorgeous green eyes from the mess her murderer left for a face. Michel choked on his whisky and coughed. Shock and grief can manifest themselves into very lame bodily reactions. He wasn't aware of those as he had not been so close to death himself.

The adultery committed by his wife was at the back of his mind now, as if it wanted to shove itself out of view. There was so much more going on to bother about a lover, but what if he was linked to the murder?

What if he was the murderer?

Michel drew a big sigh and buried his face in both of his hands and sobbed. He was finally allowing his tears to come for the first time since he had heard the morbid news. Life would never be the same again. Suddenly, paradise island seemed dark and menacing.

*

Ah Cheew fanned her flushed face vigorously. The table fan sitting next to her was blowing warm air on her. She looked restless. Nina kept on glancing at her every now and then. She was making samosas, veg and tuna ones. The radio had been airing the familiar cyclone jingle and apparently Doris was on the prowl.

Wind force 2. Cyclone class 2. For unknown reasons, cyclone names were always of the female gender. Was it because the wrath of Mother Nature could wreak more devastation? Certainly, true in real life. One doesn't want to awaken the anger of a woman. Nina was brewing all these thoughts while folding in the spiced mixture of herby peas and potatoes into the triangular *paar* (wraps) of the samosas. This is one skill Ah Cheew did teach her. She was good at it.

Ah Cheew had confided in her that she needs to consult *Matante* Marie for some soothsaying. The card reader-batteuse carte was well respected for her predictions. Better than Madame Kwok sometimes. The island had inherited a vast disguised animist following in manners of *longanis, batteur carte*, and *poosari*. Tega once told Ah Cheew and some other mates, half dunk on their rum and Blue Marlin beer, that the reason Creoles made good mediums and *longanis* is because they brought back a lot from mainland Africa.

Despite being mostly influenced from the sub Saharan coastal regions, many captured slaves were also dragged from tribes of neighbouring countries. Mix that with the Tamils and their own spirits, gods and Demigods, you've got a good pantheon of them to consult when you have a woe invading your peace, an illness which wouldn't listen to the doctor's call, or a strange happening within your own psyche. Everything had a solution.

'*Arrêt to ban zistwar* Tega!' Ah Cheew was exasperated by his ranting. Today was not a good day to have her ear. She was annoyed to have been left out of the loop by Inspector Sanjiv. She had seen him with a foreigner, chatting away and meeting twice, yet not a word from him. Her sending free top ups to their table were in vain. Ah Cheew had a bit of self-pride in her, she wasn't going to ask the inspector, she thought he owes her some allegiance, as Nina was 'hers'.

Now, the next step was to visit *Matante* Marie, at least she would tell her things that are beyond the grave. Her soothsaying was powerful, and many times they had helped Ah Cheew when she couldn't understand the cause of a crisis.

Matante Marie always had an answer.

A pale sun in the sky, with winds picking up every now and then, unexpected after almost a month of rain. It was two thirty in the afternoon and the square in front of the eatery was almost deserted; the lunchtime crowd went back to work and the day end rush hour was still a long way off.

Ah Cheew made her way to the back, and changed her clothes. Nina called after her asking if she was going out. A grumpy 'yes' was the terse reply. The young woman carried on chopping onions for cooking the next day. A taxi came and Ah Cheew hobbled along, got in and left.

After most of the day in court, Inspector Sanjiv was bored. He leaned against his colleague's car and scanned the Cathedral St Louis's square again, looking for a distraction. A Victorian fountain used to stand centre stage circled by benches and trees that would hang with flamboyant carmine blossoms, later in the year. All of that is gone now. There is a newly landscaped park but no benches for anyone to sit. It was bare and lifeless, devoid of the familiar charm of yesteryear.

Today, a bit of north wind cut across the open area and no one stayed on the wrought-iron benches for a chat. A woman and small child hurried, the child momentarily distracted by the pigeons that pecked around his feet. Those have remained constant in this vintage landscape of Port Louis. A skateboarder, ignoring the prohibitive notices, attempted flips. An old man in a plastic raincoat holding his hat tightly onto his head rushed past the other way.

Everyone had a destination to reach. The city centre is always buzzing with people in a rush. Come Sunday, all the streets are dead. Only the urban cats and dogs haunt their regular spots. Sometimes hissing or barking to shoo away an invisible enemy, but at most times enjoying a peaceful lie down.

Inspector Sanjiv had been missing Nina. He felt he was ready to pop the question to the young woman. His mood is always uplifted when he sees her. Lately, the twists of the investigation had been baffling him. Fabio has been carrying out his little visits to different spots in the capital close to the bay. The Parisian detective seemed quite upset not to be able to enjoy himself on the white stretches of beach on l'île Maurice, but instead had to carry out a beach murder investigation.

*

A bicycle had been padlocked to the parking meter.

"What would you like to drink, madame?"

There was no door or front window. The cake shop was directly onto the sidewalk. Anne Marie turned her glance away from the street to face the girl.

At this time of the morning, the Pâtisserie Providence, was hot despite the large revolving fan that stood on the refrigerator. Paper napkins fluttered on the bamboo tables when they were caught in the artificial breeze.

"Any fresh juice, *mademoiselle*?" Anne Marie enquired. The girl shook her head. A crescent of starched cotton was pinned into her hair. The hair had been straightened but a couple of unruly strands rose from behind the white cotton. She wore pink lipstick. She held an order pad in one hand, a pencil in the other. She did not look at Anne Marie or me but stared out into the street as if fascinated by the padlocked bicycle. Then she shrugged.

"Only cane juice." Anne Marie said, "Two glasses, please, with ice and a slice of lime. And a couple of cakes."

"*Ki gato mamzel*?"

Anne Marie hesitated between the line of

perfect pink cream cakes, *puits d'amour*, *tartes bananes* and custard slices.

'*Puit d'amour* and *tarte banane s'il vous plaît*"

The girl nodded and moved away, scarcely lifting her feet. The Dodo rubber sandals flapped against the floor. Her dark legs were badly blemished. Anne Marie turned to Trousseau.

"There is never any fresh juice."

"It's all imported. Madame, if you want fresh juice, real fresh fruit juice, you must come out and visit me in the country. Guava, passion fruit, bananas, pineapple, star apple, custard fruit."

She gave a short laugh of pride. "My father grows them all."

A few minutes later the girl placed the drinks on the table.

"Come and visit, you will get really fresh juice. I will personally make it for you."

The girl left a piece of paper, torn from her pad, beneath the plate and returned to her stool behind the counter, where she continued to stare at the mid-morning sunshine and the bicycle.

"I thought you lived in Port Louis"

"Yes, but I'm from the countryside, in the suburbs, madam. We live by the gentle flanks of Crève Coeur. I'm not ashamed to work with my hands, to get them dirty turning the soil.

For me, labouring the soil is nothing to be ashamed of. These days urban girls don't want to get their hands dirty. They don't want to work in the fields because they think it's beneath their dignity." She added, "Just because I have a black man's name and because my skin is dark, madam, don't think I'm afraid of hard work."

She gave her a broad, friendly smile. "Would you care for some poudine maïs cake? It's freshly made, it tastes heavenly with our own island's vanilla."

"But you like it here, don't you?"

"Yes, madam, where else can people like us go? We were born in this place and will die here too. That's our fate. Life used to be much better, but now things have become difficult. People are being killed left and right I tell you! What sort of world is this?"

"Where?"

"What? Didn't you hear? It is all over the

news. Madame Ah Cheew's eatery opposite the square, has been having inspectors, detectives and what not, I tell you.'

Anne Marie who came to this area to gather some information could not have asked for any better. This is the sort of place where gossip gathers from unknown vectors of human pourparlers.

"Soon, it will be like Haïti, with Papa Doc and *les Tontons Macoutes* running around with machine guns and machetes, that's what this island will be like."

She pointed at Anne Marie.

"You think my family will want to stay here?"

Anne Marie wiped her sticky fingers on the paper serviette. The girl was more than willing to talk. As if she was waiting for someone to start a conversation to pour out her own thoughts. She looked lonely.

A man entered the pâtisserie. Against the morning light, he formed a tall silhouette with broad shoulders and a narrow waist. He approached their table. He held out his hand. "Madame Harriet?" "I am Fabio"

The man was embarrassed. He turned to Anne Marie. "You must be...." Anne Marie nodded.

"I was at the scene when the body was discovered. It was in fact, on the beach almost in front of my house."

"I was expecting a man." A tight smile.

"Ah! ... trust you're not too disappointed."

'I generally go to the eatery you see opposite the square; lunch time is over now and there's not much there except a drink and snack if Nina has made them.'

'Nina?'

'That's the waitress, she does everything as such and it's a nice place.'

Fabio felt that investigations couldn't be carried out in a patisserie. Too much sweetness around for morbid questions. This case was proving very queer indeed.

14

Sighting

All her life, clever Ami had been a slave in the Village of the Roche-en-Pleur, a place where the sea and sky met.

She's heard the stories about the fabled People of the Sea, a people who possessed unimaginable technology who live below the waves in the dark, secret places of the ocean. She never dreamed those stories were true. When a ship emerges from the ocean and men burn her village, Ami is captured and enslaved below the waves in Mû, a world filled with ancient cities of glass and metal, floating gardens, and wondrous devices that seem to work magic. To make matters worse, her village nemesis, the chieftain's son, Mbira, is captured with her, and they are made servants in the same household beneath the sea.

Desperate to be free, Ami plots her escape, even going so far as to work with Mbira. But the sea holds more secrets than she realizes, and escape might not be as simple as leaving.

In some insignificant corner of the universe, an ocean was awaiting death. It stretched as far as the eye could see and was as calm as a lily-pond, disturbed only by a faraway spit of land, a distant and unimportant blight, a relic of a lost battle.

The ocean had long since laid claim to the

planet, swamping all mainland and leaving this rebellious mountain for no reason other than there was simply no need to conquer it; the sea and land drew their own invisible boundaries.

Although the ocean gave the pretence of tranquillity, it was, in fact, in turmoil. Following its victory against the land, there had been a glorious time of peace where all had thrived and, besides the natural competition for resources between its peoples, all had been content.

Then, something inexplicable happened.

Forces from beyond had meddled with its fragile ecosystem, shaking the pillar that supported all life and cracking the very foundations of the planet. Why or who was to blame was a complete mystery. Only one thing was certain: in the last few millions of years, their actions had upset the balance on the planet to the detriment and slow deterioration of all living beings.

The ocean, from the perspective of the casual observer, would appear to be similar to the ones found on Earth. This could not be further from the truth. When traveling between dimensions or planets, or - in the most extreme cases - both, the standard advice is to write down the rules of physics at your point of departure and then swiftly throw that information into the nearest waste disposal container.

In other words, forget everything you have learnt and start afresh. Some dimensions are kind, offering no familiarity at all, and therefore the traveller almost expects the unexpected. Others are strikingly similar yet so very different, and each difference comes as a shocking, often deadly surprise.

This particular dimension is such a place. Prior research before making a shift between dimensions is paramount. Unfortunately, such a luxury was not granted to one very confused human. Ami.

She was one of those who rekindled life in her hybrid self. She breathed underwater as well as on land. With the huge deluge that engulfed mega cities, after Shrava stole the key of the gates to the oceans from the head priestess.

However, curses follow a certain rule. They abide with that of the supreme creator. They gave in to Mother Nature. She makes life possible. Ami lived in a place that had no name. It was not even a land but one in between. She was to populate the land and evolve into humans devoid of any remnants of their aquatic past. Ami was created by the hot liquids which escaped the earth's core to cool down in the deep oceans. When the islands of the Mascarenes were formed out of undersea volcanic eruptions. They were inhabited by the people of Roche Blanche who vowed to live above the sea, among the rocks from which they get their name-a collection of bone-white shards of stone that protrude from the seawater like teeth of a rotting jawbone, sea-stained and crumbling even in their glory. The village is carved deep into the rocks like the tunnels of ants into the earth, and it glows with a thousand pinpricks of light at night when the sea and sky are dark. Travelers say it looks as though someone has folded the sky around the rocks like a blanket, and all the stars are on fire. The melody of the waves lulls the babies to sleep at night in their seaweed-fibre cradles, and the rush of the tide makes them wake in the morning. The inhabitants of Roche Blanche sing love songs about the sea, and they play in its shallows as children, but as men, they grow to fear its power and its secrets.

If only they had known how many secrets the sea held.

*

Relishing freedom after long hours indoors, Jonas dashed toward the waves and felt the bliss of the pounding surf as it lapped around his ankles, then up to his knees and waist as he dashed into the sea. The previous encounter he had in the lagoon that day had dimmed in his memory, and he had got brave again. Besides, who could resist such an inviting beach and tropical turquoise sea?

Time became irrelevant as he swam out past the breakers and into calmer waters. This was the life he had always dreamt of! He would have to find an excuse not to come here every day for his entire stay on the island. Diving beneath the waves, the immense expanse of blue encircled him. He never feels as vibrant or alive as he does when he is under the surface of the water. All the residual frustrations he felt washed away with each wave crashing over him. With a grin on his face, he challenged himself to dive as deeply as he could before coming up for air.

Enveloping him each time he dived beneath the surface were silvery fish, darting here and there in small schools. Every time he drew near them, they skittered off just beyond the reach of his fingertips. Playfully, he would swim into them, making them break apart only to re-join later. Once bored with the fish, he swam further out to sea and was astonished to see a sea turtle hovering not far from him. The methodically serene flapping of its fins as if it were a bird in the sky caught his attention, as he watched it glide past, bouncing slightly with each stroke. Breaking the surface with a large gulp of air, he flipped over onto his back and floated for a while.

The rays of the midday sun shone down on him with a comforting warmth that contrasted to the cool waters beneath him. He floated for a while before rolling onto his stomach and letting himself tread water for a bit. Trudging along with the incoming waves, he splayed across the wavelets, rocking his body, arms spread out like an albatross. Just when his body started to relax, he heard what sounded like the soft purr of an engine. Propping himself up, he gazed out across the water to see a guy riding a watercraft that resembled a Jet Ski.

Creasing his eyebrows, he pushed himself up to a standing position and glided over to where it seemed like the guy was heading. Stumbling over rocks and slipping on slimy algae, he made it over to the rocky outcroppings when the guy disembarked the watercraft. He watched him curiously, as he pulled the craft up beyond the reaches of the surf. He clearly hadn't noticed Jonas watching him yet, but when he did, he jumped with a start.

"Hey, who are you and what are you doing here?" he questioned, stomping up the sandy bank to where he stood next to a cluster of mussel encrusted rocks. His outfit resembled that of a space suit, minus the helmet. Blue outlines trailed the seams along with matching blue insignias on each arm. Messy-blond hair hung shabbily past his slightly big ears and touched the tips of his mid-level cheekbones. "Hey, why don't you answer me? How did you get here? I didn't see you when I left."

The guy looked at Jonas with quizzical eyes, as if was trying to size him up, to determine what kind of person he was.

"What are you doing here?" He pushed back, staring right back at him, defiantly.

*

"I'm here to collect data like I always do." The guy looked him up and down, examining him like he was an alien species.

He glanced out to sea and stated, "I have to go."

"What?" "I need to return to Mû. I will come back, don't worry. And don't say anything to anyone else about me."

He raced down the beach to his watercraft, tossing his right leg over the seat while entering a code on the touchscreen. The engine roared to life and the front control panel began to light up. Jonas could swear he heard him mumble in addition, "Or what you're about to see."

Before he could make up his mind to say something, he sped off on the waves. The scientist watched him go until something odd happened. Perhaps he blinked his eyes or experienced some weird sea mirage, but he simply vanished. No, not just vanish; he disappeared underneath the waves...and never resurfaced. Bewildered, Jonas sat on one of the rocks and waited until the last orange rays of sunset faded into a dark blue, he never returned.

Nor did he ever see him resurface.

Perplexed, Jonas slowly made his way to the fence of the resort's boundary. He began to think about what he'd just seen. Either he was dreaming or the stranger had drowned and died. None of it seemed real. It was furthering what he had experienced that day on the beach when the junkie urged him to go back to the hotel.

How could someone simply disappear into the ocean and not resurface?

As he meandered to his room, he continued to ponder the various possibilities, his thoughts encumbered by the strangeness of his day. It was impossible that anyone could survive for hours without surfacing to breathe. Maybe his crazy sea-space suit had a regulator and ample oxygen attached.

No, that didn't make any sense.

The outfit was too tight fitting to contain such accessories. Something was weird about the man and maybe the beach too. It didn't matter. He would keep returning to that beach until he ran into him again. If what he said were true, he would definitely return.

Yes, he was bound to return and when he did, Jonas would be there. He didn't care how long he had to wait. He was inching towards a theory which had been peeking in his head. That there was a place that was habitable under the sea.

But where? Jonas heard him say Mû ... did he? Bewildered, Jonas tossed his thoughts around making himself believe he really didn't hear the word Mû ... if it was, then ...it would be explosive!

« *Look, our distant ancestors most likely evolved in Asia, in a hothouse world newly free of dinosaurs. More than 55 million years ago, in the lush rainforests of what is now east Asia, a new voice was heard in the animal chorus: the cry of the first primate.*

Archicebus Achilles is the earliest primate skeleton ever found. It also strongly suggests that our lineage evolved in Asia, several million years earlier than we thought, and links the evolution of primates to the most extreme episode of climate change of the last 65 million years.

It dates from 55 million years ago, has the relatively small eyes of an animal active during the day and the sharp molar teeth of an insect-eater. Significantly, it also has the hind limbs and flexible foot of a primate that had already taken to leaping between branches *and gripping them with its feet – characteristics that we lost only when our ancestors left the trees just a few million years ago. In fact, a 2013 study revealed that at least 1 in 13 of us still has a flexible foot – a trait, it seems, that may be traceable all the way back to an animal very like Archicebus. The first analysis of Archicebus placed it, not on our direct line, but with our next-door neighbours, the tarsiers of south-east Asia. However, it is hard to say for sure which group it belongs to. There is one main reason for believing that Archicebus is closer to home. Parts of its body are eerily similar to what we would expect to find in our oldest ancestor. Its ankle bone, in particular, looks just like a monkey's – a feature that led the team to name the remarkable fossil after the Greek hero Achilles. Perhaps most significantly, the fossil supports the idea that primates originated in South East Asia and suggests that the ancestors of all monkeys and apes had already split off from other primates 55 million years ago – millions of years earlier than textbooks suggest. This links the birth of our primate line to a major spike in global temperatures known as the Palaeocene-Eocene Thermal Maximum (PETM). It also puts our point of origin squarely in the heart of the PETM furnace: equatorial Asia.*

Primates are well adapted to the tropics, so it makes sense that they originated in a warm climate. What's more, South East Asia would have offered a refuge for tropical species to weather the storm of cooler times: while the Earth's drifting tectonic plates dragged all major continents across the latitudes, this region remained where it was, right on the equator. Many ecological niches were open for the taking after the great mass extinction, and the hot climate would have produced plenty of insects and fruit. However, this leaves us with a puzzle. As we will see in later chapters, Africa was the cradle of humanity, so at some point early monkey-like primates must have moved from Asia over to Africa: perhaps sometime around 40 million years ago. This is hard to explain, because at that time the vast Tethys Sea separated Asia and Africa. Monkey archaeology, if you trace the family history of primates, monkeys are somewhere in the middle: further along than the oldest groups like lemurs but not as human-like as the apes.

Yet they have achieved something truly remarkable. In 2016 the first 'monkey archaeology' dig uncovered the tools used by previous generations of wild macaques – a group of primates separated from humans by some 25 million years of evolution. The discovery means that humans aren't alone in leaving a record of past culture that can be pried open by archaeology. All sorts of animals can use tools, but they are usually made from perishable materials like leaves and twigs. This makes the origin of this behaviour difficult to study, but Burmese long-tailed macaques are a rare exception. They are renowned for their use of stone tools to crack open shellfish, crabs and nuts, making them one of the very few primates that have followed hominins into the Stone Age.

Michael Haslam at the University of Oxford and his team conducted the dig on the small *island of Paik Nam Yei in Thailand, one of the islands where the monkeys live and use stone tools. They sifted through the sandy sediments at the site and found ten stone tools attributed to macaques, based on their wear patterns.*

By dating the oyster shells found in the same sediment layers, they determined that the tools could be as old as 65 years, going back two macaque generations. We know from eyewitness accounts that these monkeys have been using tools for at least 120 years, so the study doesn't push the age of the behaviour back. But Haslam sees it as a first step towards digging deeper into the origins of the behaviour. Exactly how far back in time the macaques' Stone Age extends is anyone's guess. A rare 'chimpanzee archaeology' dig in the early 2000s showed that chimps have been using stone tools for more than 4,000 years.

Today, most apes are relatively rare and isolated. Chimpanzees and gorillas are confined to a few small patches of Africa, while orangutans are found only on Borneo and Sumatra. Only gibbons roam more widely. Yet if you could look back in time to between 20 and 7 million years ago, science fiction was science fact: The Earth really was the planet of the apes.

At least a hundred species roamed the world before the first humans appeared. They were remarkable in number and diversity, but are more fascinating still for what they tell us about our own origins. Key human traits – including big brains, dexterous hands, erect posture and long childhood – can be traced back to this period. The really surprising thing is that these features all evolved in European apes.

There is no doubt that apes originated in Africa, or that our more recent evolution happened there. But for a time between these two landmarks, apes hovered on the verge of extinction on their home continent while flourishing in Europe.

What's more, the transformation of European species during this time made us who we are. Line them up in your head. Generation after generation of your ancestors, reaching back in time through civilizations, ice ages, an epic migration out of Africa, to the very origin of our species. And on the other side, take a chimp and line up its ancestors. How far back do you have to go, how many generations have to pass, before the two lines meet? New estimates for when our lineage and chimps went their separate ways suggest that some of our established ideas are staggeringly wrong.

If these suggestions are correct, they demand a rewrite of human prehistory, starting from the very beginning. I believe that there was a certain time when men lived as sophisticated beings and created great things, but a huge part of it has been wiped out. »

Jonas closed the book, he had just read. Checking and refreshing his memory about the origins of man.

Mû in all of this was like a surreal bubble.

Too good to be true.

Too scary of it was true.

15

Shanti Villa

Fabio Grignon called upon Jonas for some questions. The scientist didn't come to him as being very clear about his theories. However, he finally could talk to a man who not only had a keen ear for his explanations but was also investigating a murder case. It was the body recovered on the beach.

Could any of this provide an explanation to Jonas' recent strange encounters?

'You want to say that you saw a man

disappear in the sea and not resurface?'

'Yes indeed, and I believe there's something else going on under the sea. You should investigate what the murdered scientist was working on.' Fabio looked at Jonas for a moment and blew some loops of smoke in the air.

Somewhere, the scientist had struck a chord. Instead of finding a plausible murder by stereotype elimination methods, why not dig deeper?

'Yes, you are right, I shall start an inquiry upon the research gate Dr Ducasse was working at, maybe there is something else out there. Alright then, let me take leave now. It was a pleasure meeting you.'

'The pleasure was all mine ... and don't forget to keep me informed, should you receive any information. Remember I am only a scientist, I would like to understand history, archaeology and what comes with it. It is very sad to lose a fellow scientist like Dr Valériane Ducasse.'

The two men bid each other goodbye, while the sun shrouded itself in a mass of clouds. Jonas felt a strange chill and made his way back to his room.

There's a special word for anybody who drives a car in Baie du Tombeau: tourist.

Locals ride bicycles. But even if you're sober, the way to reach home is walking. Easy enough for any drunk.

Riding a bicycle is pretty straightforward. You lean half-forward, drape one forearm over the handlebars, and slouch over in a kind of boneless way while your legs move on the pedals as if you were going downhill and you're just keeping up with the spinning wheel; you're not really pedalling at all, just letting gravity pull you along. It works out pretty well on an island that's completely flat and only a few miles long and a few miles across.

Petrol is expensive, and unless you're hauling lumber, cars are a waste of time and money and take up too much room. Besides, nobody is really in a hurry here, but they often pretend to be. It heightens their sense of importance.

Tourists are here for a break from the hectic rodent marathon. Residents generally don't have anything too pressing; at worst, they're keeping a tourist waiting a few minutes, which is actually one of the real pleasures of living here, so nobody minds. Most are haggling to hustle some more business.

Like you know where they would like to visit, you then push forward to be their guide, provide transport. They are nearing lunch or dinner, then come to this 'amazing' place with authentic Mauritian food which you stress on the 100%! Always works. Food and transport have kept men on the move for thousands of years.

*

Inspector Sanjiv sat on a bench by the beach and observed a couple of locals with some tourists. They had stopped to check on some *paréos* which are really attractive in their bright island style motifs and colours. He had been entrusted to 'know' a little more about what goes near the most popular part of the beach where Valériane's body was found.

Usually, a vast residential area where once

redundant stevedores took refuge after the '*vrac terminale*' in Les Salines. Ever since, with their meagre compensation, they built shacks with tin sheets which got blown each year with the strongest gusts of during the cyclonic weather. Nowadays, they have smartened a bit and hustle on the side with all sorts of entrepreneurial small businesses. Many also go bust after a few months when their drinking overtakes their good will.

Inspector Sanjiv grilling a last cigarette wondered who would come here to kill a high-profile Caucasian woman? For he had had the last report from Fabio that Valériane Ducasse indeed worked for one of the richest labs in Europe. She was conducting some research on the island for some years now.

But on what? No details.

The Inspector got up from the beach bench

and ventured towards the gato pima seller, there was a waft of roti in the air. Probably some fresh ones being cooked. This reminded him of Nina. His Nina. It made him smile.

Deep inside, Sanjiv had already ventured to the next level of his relationship with the young widow. She was living by his side, washing his clothes, taking his belt away when he came from work, making him fresh *rotis* with *rougay, cari gros pois* and *zasar*. The fib of his imagination ran in a flash, but sadly that brightness was lacklustre when it came to investigating this murder. He knew the limitations of his prowess.

He said it, then. Home. This was home. This was Shanti Villa – the Place of Peace, the name Valériane had chosen for their home. Home, a sacred word.

The only home he'd ever known. A sprawling garden of white sand paths weaving between beds of canna lilies and hibiscus bushes and pink oleander. Wooden trellises up the side of the house bursting with bunches of bougainvillea in purple, shocking pink, bright red. Explosions of colours wherever eyes roamed, so vivid and clashing; or else the restful green above, of trees through which sunlight filtered, the green palms of coconut trees towering against the vibrant blue of the sky, tall and thin, majestic and uniquely Mauritian.

Home was this house, a cool bungalow nestled within all this abundant foliage, shaded by two mango trees on one side and a tamarind on the other and a flamboyant tree to the front that dropped its brilliant blooms at the entrance to form a red carpet during the hot months.

To the entrance of the low staircase leading up to the wide veranda that wrapped the house in a cool ribbon of serenity, cooled by the sea breezes that drifted in from the east, were fragrant roses, jasmine and frangipanis. The grounds were spacious, extending back into a woodland area left untended; just as they both loved it. There was also a patch of vegetable garden where Raju the gardener grew herbs, tomatoes, brinjal, chilies and some mustard greens. He came and went, looking after the plants, leaving the harvests on the kitchen table. No one asked any questions.

Michel and Valériane Ducasse considered this place as their own *'havre de paix'*. Though each lived in their own minds, they met on regular intervals to soak in the silent garden on their deck chairs sipping a chilled passion fruit juice when it got too hot.

Michel had been going through his late wife's office trying to find a clue to anything that could lead to her murderer. He tumbled over the pencil holder in a vase, out rolled a tiny round plastic box. He opened it, a soft cotton ball was inside. He carefully unrolled it and there was a shiny object. Like a diamond in the form of a scale.

'What is this? A diamond? Can't be ... Valériane hated jewellery, especially anything sparkly.'

He remembered that she kept to her gold wedding band. That was all she ever wore. So where does this gem come from?

He turned it around and there was no sign of any hook, to disclose that it could be a pendant, an earring ...hmm strange! He went to the left side of the room where sat 3 digital microscopes. He carefully inserted the object on one of the plates and adjusted the lens. It shone brightly under the light. Well too brightly in fact. Michel pulled away, and blinked his eyes for a second, taking a rest from the flash. He went back again and this time steadied his gaze. What he detected was even more astounding. It seemed that there was minuscule bright diamond like gems which made up one larger one.

A light lens flare gave them a rainbow-like iridescence.

Suddenly, something caught his attention. The stones were moving. Like cells. He pulled out his eyes from the microscope.

'What the hell is this?' He muttered to himself. A mynah flew by the window singing melodiously. As if all was right in this garden of Eden, but all wasn't well. What revealed itself under the lens of the microscope was most unsettling. Could this be a reason why Valériane kept quiet? What was it? Has she discovered something more astounding that the eye could see?

Outside a Bengali sang in a mellifluous tone rivalling that of the mynah, probably feeling happy. Michel kept on looking at the shiny object, and kept thinking if it was really of any importance or just the result of a confused mind.

Valériane usually told him about any major turn in her research, but she mentioned nothing of having this strange object. He looked in her canvas tote, found her purse and opened it. Inside was a picture of them when they got married. She always said she liked it very much, for it shows us 'happy and hopeful for our future'. There were some Mauritian currency notes, a few credit cards, and some bits of paper. One of them was the address of a jeweller in Rose Hill.

'So, you did go to investigate this peculiar object?' he said to himself

Michel poured himself a cold glass of Blue Marlin beer and went to sit on his favourite deck chair.

The other one stayed painfully empty.

A deep orange red sun began to set close to the horizon, descending toward its daily trek across the heavens; the sky slowly transformed into a myriad of colours at every passing minute of the bright orb's leisurely procession. The deep reds and oranges of the sunset dissolved into a stunning mottled spread, dotted with strands of cotton-like clouds.

Beneath the majestic sky lay an emerald-green turning into shimmers of the flame, an ocean so still, that it resembled a solid piece of glass, with only a few flecks of some ripples. A beautiful sight to behold. Mauritius is surrounded by beaches of soft, bleached white sand. It looked as if someone had laid a barrier of flour around the entire island. The shoreline was contiguous and served as a buffer between the depth of the sea and the island's Southern smooth-faced cliffs. From where Michel sat, his melancholy tinged with grief guided his thoughts towards the cause of his beautiful wife having been so brutally killed.

Life is shocking when it reels off its ugly side to you.

There is no escaping that, only time will give him solace.

For now, he needs to find why Valériane was killed, and of course, by whom?

If there are two ways that Hindus and Chinese are similar is how they observe mourning someone. They wear white. In Mauritius, a white woolly pom-pom in the hair shows that the person is mourning.

Ah Cheew arrived with a white pom-pom attached to her blouse. Nina was surprised. She had not heard of anyone recently deceased in her boss' family.

'Who has died Madame?' She asked leaning forward to show her concern.

'Who? ... don't you know?' Came a wry reply from Ah Cheew checking on the latest news from the Chinese daily which appears first thing on her counter every morning.

'I don't know, that's why I'm asking, you would have said something ...'

'That woman ... how brutally killed! Shouldn't we be all mourning her death? I have not heard anyone doing so, and yet, it happened not far from here. In fact, we need to show our respect. Anyway, that's how we Chinese do it.'

'Haan, OK Madame' replied Nina, busy folding wontons.

She prepared them in a variety of ways: on skewers, as salad cups, fried, steamed, and of course, in soup. She sampled a couple of varieties herself... for research, and found that she was a fan of steamed wontons in chili sauce in a broth with bok choy and choy sum greens. Thinking about them made her mouth water.

Ah Cheew had taught her well. How to mix and knead the dough to the correct elasticity. When rolled out, they should stretch paper thin and not break. As for the broth, Nina had to try several times to get the seasoning well, and keep the dosage of garlic, fragrant and flavourful. Ah Cheew said 'it's the broth which makes a good wonton soup, besides a good wonton, of course'.

Tega breezed in hailing a loud greeting to Ah Cheew and Nina.

'You are early today Tega, what's up?'

The middle-aged man didn't reply but asked for a Coke. Ah Cheew left him to his corner and carried on scanning her Chinese daily. A few minutes later, Tega walks to the counter.

'Who has died, Ah Cheew?'

'There we go ...' replied Ah Cheew, not lifting her head from her newspaper.

'Am only asking.... any relative?'

'No, why?'

'Well, your *barette* with the white pom-pom, isn't it a sign of grieving?'

Ah Cheew kept quiet. She was not in the mood for replying to Tega. Nina left the kitchen and came out to the counter. She could hear all the conversation. Wiping off her hands in her apron, she smiled at Tega and said softly 'Madame is wearing this because of the lady who was killed. She was after all, part of this community, right?'

Tega stared at Nina speechless and looked at Ah Cheew who blushed slightly while still pretending to read. Some days, she wished people did not talk. She had even decided she would go to the temple to light some incense and ask Buddha to appease the roaming spirit. Inspector Sanjiv had told her that the body was still in the morgue.

Definitely not at peace. Ah Cheew belonged to the generation of Chinese who still kept to old traditions. When a person dies, the spirit has to be sent off pompously with all the right offerings so that it does not roam around and annoy those still alive. She remembers that her parents' house had the threshold risen high, so that spirits do not enter the house. It is believed that they travel horizontally, hence barring the way at the threshold would stop them.

Tega bent forward to Ah Cheew, whispering 'Madame Ah Cheew it is a thoughtful thing to do, not many people are so sensitive, these days.'

Ah Cheew nodded her head, still refusing to face Tega. She had not thought about what to say to people who would ask her questions. She felt she needed to wear a sign of bereavement and that's what she did ... so naturally. Nina felt so proud of Ah Cheew, besides her nature, she has her own ways to be so apart from anyone she knows. Nina had to acknowledge that her aging boss was a force to reckon with, a true fighter.

Tega kept on sipping his Coke with a pensive look on his face. Ah Cheew finally lifted her gaze from her newspaper and caught the fleeting melancholy in Tega's face.

'So, missing someone Tega?'

"Have you ever seen the ocean at night, Ah Cheew?

'No, I always go to the beach when the sun is shining, why would I go at night? Am not a *pêcheur homard.*'

Tega turned and looked at her, 'let me recite you a few lines from my favourite book: 'The darkness seems to swallow it entirely at first glance, but after a closer look the ocean simply fools the observer. Its waves continue to crash just as strong. Its white tops continue to soak the nearby rocks. On an ethereal moonlit night, the waves illuminate the water like a flashlight streaming through a dense forest.

The human heart is as vast and complex as the ocean. Our experiences and relationships aren't always black and white, and oftentimes we only realize it when we look back. It's a wonderful thing to be able to remember your precious moments long after they've passed. All those emotions flood back with each memory. Those precious moments are locked away deep in your subconscious like a forgotten shipwreck at the bottom of the ocean floor away from the light of day for years and years. Then, one day, they float to the top and reveal themselves just as clearly as when you experienced them the first time.'

'I did not know that you were so poetic Tega, one needs a decent memory to remember such lines, how come you are just a stevedore?'.

'Destiny Ah Cheew, ...just my fate. I loved literature, history and arts but my parents didn't survive cyclone Gervaise, they both drowned in Rivière du Pouce while trying to rescue someone. I will tell you how I met the woman I would remember for the rest of my life. People come and go in your life throughout the years, but few truly stay in your heart and mind permanently. Those are the people you were meant to meet, and their impact will stay with you long after they're gone from your life. The simplest thing will remind you of them. Some think it's a curse to remember someone who's no longer there, but I think it's a gift. You will replay those happy moments over and over again, sometimes remembering the tiniest detail. It allows you the pleasure of reliving them again, ever so briefly.'

Ah Cheew cowed into her famous gentle smile, seemingly content to have Tega confide in her.

'You know Ah Cheew, despite having lost my sweetheart, I simply could never erase her from my heart. Humans are like that, aren't they? Be around and you are taken for granted. Once you lose someone, your brain adjusts your memories to match your beliefs, and you may as well be a bug on a tree shifting around to follow your shadow.'

'Wow! Tega you have really surprised me today! I want to hear more.'

'That's all for now, my grandma is unwell, I have to take her to the dispensary.'

Tega put some coins on the counter and left.

16

The Dream

It was the same dream. Quiet whisperings that morphed hauntingly into the morning easily, as if another world claimed her too. Her hands and feet were bound, entangled in a thick web of vine, and all attempts to break loose only exhausted her.

The creeping weeds grew thicker, tighter, and reduced her movement to the pulsation of blood and the rapid blink of an eye. Particles of pungent earth clogged her nostrils and choked her throat, making it hard to breathe. Her heart thumped, ricocheting inside her chest. Abruptly, the scene shifted. She was now enclosed on all four sides.

Above, a dark wooden ceiling; below, two-inch thick oak flooring supported her weight. There was room now to move her hands and feet, and her airways were clear. She drew in a full breath. Rays of light flickered through a tiny crack. Suddenly, the ceiling flew off the enclosure followed by the front, back, left and right walls. She clung to the wooden flooring that floated in a vast empty space. If she let go, she feared a plunge into an inky abyss. Her fingers tightened around the edge of the wooden floor.

She had been here many times before. This time, slowly, reluctantly, she peeled her fingers open one by one until only her thumb and forefinger clutched the wooden plank. With a sharp exhale, she released. Awareness expanded to merge with an undefined dimension and immense open possibility. Solid forms arose from the void to populate the emptiness like endless stars fading in and out. A lone bumblebee crawled across the surface of a sunflower, fractals and geometric patterns spiralling. The insect sensed for the perfect location to extract nectar in a symbiotic relationship inherent within the whole of creation. The sweet smell of dew and a crystalline sharpness filled the air. Images streamed in chromatic intensity, one after the other. Dozens of humming birds hover in mid-air like tiny ornaments reflecting spectral light. A lake appeared, and clouds echoed on the mirrored surface. Dragonflies skated across the calm water. The girl advanced across a meadow toward an emerald lake where a white elephant frolicked, showering itself in a bubbly spray.

The girl held out her hand as if she might reach across the meadow and touch the elephant's trunk. In a blink, the elephant morphed, minuscule now, no taller than her index finger, all four of its feet firmly planted in the centre of her palm, its pale eyelashes curling in an arc. She lifted her hand to see. There was a pure gold anklet with a tiny mermaid charm on one of the elephant's hind feet. The elephant raised its tiny trunk and probed the girl's eyes, nose, and chin and blew its warm breath into her ear.

She giggled. The elephant's skin was rough and prickly and made the hair on her arm rise and tingle.

Once again, the scene shifted abruptly. She found herself towering four metres above the earth, sitting precariously on the pachyderm's skin, directly behind its large ears, which securely pinned her legs. Every so often, the elephant opened its ears, and the girl quickly laid her head down, tightening her arms on its neck. It moved towards the water, eased into it, and then began to swim.

Beyond the lake towered a pagoda with a golden roof and stones of turquoise, red, and black. The air was suffused with jasmine while light bells tinkled in the crisp mountain air. The girl and the elephant were both intent on swimming to the other side. Superimposed, the rounded eyes of a jaguar watched, his whiskers vibrating with the elephant's strokes.

Then, all faded, blurred and unconscious darkness wiped all images. Gululethu was now sleeping soundly.

The turquoise ocean lapped gently onto Grand Baie, contrasting sharply against the brilliant cerulean sky. Bleached clouds hugged the horizon, but the upper atmosphere remained luminous and clear, apart from a wisp of a cirrus. Palm and casuarina trees wavered in the light breeze as several groups of well-conditioned and scantily clad youth played volleyball along the shore.

From his Hawaiian style shirt, now popular with Mauritian tourists, and tailored khaki pants to dark sunglasses, Fabio was just as well dressed as the shorter man walking beside him, their heads bent together in deep conversation.

Professor Jonas was meeting the French detective for the second time, but it felt as if they had always known each other.

'Jonas you reckon that this small island sits on the oldest continent the world has ever known! Many theories about the origins of man will soon be thwarted into absurd scientific chaos.'

'Indeed, the planet is much older than we think, and historical theories may need to be re-written. Nothing we have compiled is non-refutable. It is the work of science to challenge, probe, investigate and make new discoveries.'

'How about the diamond connection?' whispered Fabio.

'So, it is! I have evidence.' Jonas looked at him with wide keen blue eyes.

'Would you say that all the beautiful turquoise sea we have around the island is full of gems?'

'Much more of the expanse of this island and its territorial waters. It encompasses nearly all of the Indian Ocean.'

'Phew! That's incredible! ...if it was proven to be true.'

'Slowly ...slowly the truth will surface.'

'You really believe it could well be a secret the lab Professor Ducasse was working for, held in utter confidentiality?'

'I believe so, and the local authorities have no clue about it?! That's simply hard to believe!'.

'Well, small young insular nations often are struck by such realities, their red taped system is still very archaic. They haven't learnt to assume their responsibility to any foreign company set up here. You see, it's a sad postcolonial syndrome.

Locals will hesitate to question a white man.'

'But we have a murder to solve Jonas. And I need your help. Anything you can enlighten me with to provide a lead toward real justice.'

'Yes, I am trying Fabio … am trying.'

Both men arrived at the parking lot, Fabio opened the door to his rented SUV and Jonas got in.

Within a short drive, they reached the inner suburb of the capital and parked in one of the small cobbled streets. The sun was high up at its zenith and that meant many passers-by were heading towards a shady part to enjoy a bit of lunch.

Jonas and Fabio opened Ah Cheew's door and were welcomed by the homely atmosphere and a strong waft of delicious food being cooked. The place was almost full, but they found themselves a table for four and sat there sheepishly, feeling a bit guilty to occupy more than two places. A slim and tall woman with a demure smile came to them, and handed them a laminated sheet of the menu.

'Bonjour, this is the menu, we have *salmi poulet*, fried rice, wonton soup, *bol renversé*, *baguette* with liver stir fry, *achar légumes* and *vindaye ourite*.'

'I will have the baguette with vindaye please and some fresh juice!'

Fabio took a few seconds to make his choice and decided upon a safer and familiar choice.

'I will have a baguette with liver please and a Coke with lots of ice please!'

Nina memorized the order and came back within minutes with their drinks. The two started their conversation.

'So, where was I?'

'You were to give me clues and evidence to elucidate this murder ...'

'Oh right! ... well you need to understand certain key points though ...'

Fabio internally raised his eyes saying to himself 'here, we go again with professor Jonas' theories.'

Jonas started his monologue to a very attentive Fabio, who took notes while listening.

'The memory of nature is in reality a stupendous unity, a Gaia. As in another way, all humankind is found to constitute a spiritual unity if we ascend to a sufficiently elevated plane of nature in search of the wonderful convergence where unity is reached without the loss of individuality. For ordinary humanity, however, at the early stage of its evolution represented by the majority, the interior spiritual capacities ranging beyond those which the brain is an instrument for expressing, are as yet too imperfectly developed to enable them to get in touch with any other records in the vast archives of nature's memory, except those with which they have individually been in contact at their creation.'

'Hang on ... do you mean that as a scientist, you validate clairvoyance?' Fabio interrupted, his curiosity piqued.

'What do you mean to me, as a scientist? Of course, I do, we all do. Certain scientists do not want to validate it as they consider them as dark or occult arts. Remember that witches were persecuted and burnt as promulgating heresy, in fact, it was divination, alchemy and deep knowledge. Men who wanted to control people and enjoy this power had to get rid of all those who proved them wrong.

So, yes astral clairvoyance has given tremendous insights to what hard science was unable to provide men with hard evidence.

There is no limit, really, to the resources of astral clairvoyance in investigations concerning the past history of the earth, whether we are concerned with the events that have befallen the human race in prehistoric epochs, or with the growth of the planet itself through geological periods which pre-dated the advent of man, or with more recent events, current narrations of which have been distorted by careless or perverse historians. The memory of Mother Nature is infallibly accurate and inexhaustibly minute.

A time will come as certainly as the precession of the equinoxes, when the literary method of historical research will be laid aside, as out of date, in the case of all original work.'

'Yet how does all that relate to our murder mystery?' pondered Fabio, more and more interested by Jonas' exposé. He was certainly not expecting to reach such turns.

Nina brought two plates of baguette which were attractively filled and appetizing.

'Here we go, *bon appétit messieurs!*'

'*Merci*' replied both in unison. Fabio started his baguette, but Jonas still had more to say.

'*Mmm ...c'est trop bon*! Try yours'

'*Oui ...oui* so good, I was saying that I do think that we have our answers from some well-known astral clairvoyance practitioners.'

'How is that so?'

'Well, you see science depends on exactitude and inference. But astral clairvoyance gives us more information than we would like to accept.'

Fabio encouraged Jonas to have a bite, having a respite sort of way... but Jonas kept on talking.

'Hundreds of thousands of years which elapsed from the time when the earliest Aryans left their home on the shores of central Asia to the time of the Greeks and Romans, bore witness to the rise and fall of innumerable civilizations. Of the 1st sub-race of our Aryan Race who inhabited India and colonial Egypt in prehistoric times we know practically nothing, and the same may be said of the Chaldean, Babylonian, and Assyrian nations who composed the 2nd sub-race—for the fragments of knowledge obtained from the recently deciphered hieroglyphs or cuneiform inscriptions on Egyptian tombs or Babylonian tablets can scarcely be said to constitute a comprehensive history.

The Persians who belonged to the 3rd or Iranian sub-race have, it is true, left a few more traces, but

of the earlier civilizations of the Keltic or 4th sub-race we have no records at all. It is only with the rise of the last family shoots of this Keltic stock, viz., the Greek and Roman peoples, that we come upon historic times.

In addition to the blank period of the past, there is an obvious blank period in the future. Of the seven sub-races required to complete the history of a great Root Race, five only have so far come into existence. Our own Teutonic or 5th sub-race has already developed many nations, but has not yet run its course, while the 6th and 7th sub-races, who will be developed on the continents of North and South America, will have thousands of years of history to give to the world.'

'Where do you place the Indian Ocean in all of this with reference to your last talk, remember?'

'That's it my friend! This is where it gets more interesting.'

Finally, the morsel of baguette with vindaye reached his mouth, and he took a pause.

Fabio was most enchanted, there was a way to stop the professor.

'Hmmm, this is most delicious!' exclaimed the professor looking for the waitress to compliment her, but Nina was busy in the kitchen. However, Ah Cheew had not let the two men out of her vision, although Jonas couldn't detect it.

'The destruction of Atlantis was accomplished by a series of catastrophes varying in character from great cataclysms in which whole territories and populations perished, to comparatively unimportant landslides such as occur on our own coasts to-day. When the destruction was once inaugurated by the first great catastrophe there was no interruption of the minor landslides which continued slowly but steadily to eat away at the continent. Four of the great catastrophes stand out in magnitude above all the rest.

The first took place in the Miocene age, about 800,000 years ago. The second, which was of minor importance, occurred about 200,000 years ago. The third—about 80,000 years ago—was a very great one. It destroyed all that remained of the Atlantean continent, with the exception of the island to which Plato gave the name of Poseidonis, which in its turn was submerged in the fourth and final great catastrophe of 9,564 B.C.E

Now the testimony of the oldest writers and of modern scientific research alike bear witness to the existence of an ancient continent occupying the site of the lost Atlantis.

Before proceeding to the consideration of the subject itself, it is proposed cursorily to glance at the generally known sources which supply corroborative evidence. These may be grouped into the five following classes: First, the testimony of the deep-sea soundings. Second, the distribution of fauna and flora. Third, the similarity of language and of ethnological type.

Fourth, the similarity of religious belief, ritual, and architecture.

Fifth, the testimony of ancient writers, of early race traditions, and of archaic flood-legends.

In the first place, then, the testimony of the deep-sea soundings may be summarized in a few words. Thanks chiefly to the expeditions of the British and American gunboats, "Challenger" and "Dolphin" (though Germany also was associated with this scientific exploration) the bed of the whole Atlantic Ocean is now mapped out, with the result that an immense bank or ridge of great elevation is shown to exist in mid-Atlantic.'

Some more munching of their respective baguettes provided a well-deserved interlude.

This ridge stretches in a south-westerly direction from about fifty degrees north towards the coast of South America, then in a south-easterly direction towards the coast of Africa, changing its direction again near Ascension Island, and running due south to Tristan D'Cunha. The ridge rises almost sheer about 9,000 feet from the ocean depths around it, while the Azores, St. Paul, Ascension, and Tristan D'Cunha are the peaks of this land which still remain above water. A line of 3,500 fathoms, or say, 21,000 feet, is required to sound the deepest parts of the Atlantic, but the higher parts of the ridge are only a hundred to a few hundred fathoms beneath the sea. The soundings too showed that the ridge is covered with volcanic debris of which traces are to be found right across the ocean to the American coasts.

Indeed, the fact that the ocean bed, particularly about the Azores, has been the scene of volcanic disturbance on a gigantic scale, and that within a quite measurable period of geologic time, is conclusively proven by the investigations made during the above-named expeditions.'

Fabio was going to ask why he was even talking of Atlantis, since last time he mentioned Kumari Kandam and Mû, but Fabio knew there was no point stopping the professor. Better understand what he was saying. The lunching crowd was thinning, many were re-joining their offices. Nina came to Jonas and Fabio's table to check if they needed anything more.

'Everything's alright? Would you like … OK I leave you Messieurs' noticing the almost intact baguette of Jonas. Fabio gave her a quick smile acquiescing to being left alone to finish their meals.

When Nina left, Jonas had stopped talking and started having mouthfuls of his lunch with yellow vindaye oil squishing from the side of the baguette. As if the presence of Nina was like a motherly 'stop talking and have your lunch!'

'Watch out!' But it was too late. A drop of the spicy yellow mustard oil reached Jonas' shirt. It showed itself as a bright neon sign hailing rather ungraciously 'hey attention… *Vindaye* oil! Jonas was the least bothered.

'Never mind, Marie Ange at the hotel laundry will remove it.' He excused himself looking at the stark yellow blot. It suggested that a few of such mishaps had happened before to this professor.

'Jonas I am afraid I have a meeting after lunch at the Line Barracks, we will have to stop here. But don't worry, our conversation will continue soon. How about a Zoom session tonight? What do you think?'

Jonas made a move to get up, but was stopped by Fabio who gallantly offered to pay the bill. He bid goodbye to the professor and left in a hurry shouting 'au revoir' towards Ah Cheew. Jonas kept on eating, his eyes staring in emptiness.

Ah Cheew waiting for her moment, prowled towards him. She was brewing some questions and keen to open her mouth. She had seen the handsome Frenchman before with Inspector Sanjiv, and she was sure that today's lunch meeting had something to do with the murder case. Waddling her way to the table of Jonas, Ah Cheew prepared her largest smile which made her eyes close completely giving her the look of a happy Buddha with a face as round as the moon.

'Bonjour, all is well, Monsieur?' waking Jonas from his reverie. He was surprised to see Ah Cheew and muttered a hasty but cautious 'Yes'.

'I have seen you with Monsieur Fabio who came with Inspector Sanjiv, a regular here. Are you his friend too?'

'Er ...no, but I have met him.'

'Right, it is so unfortunate that my cook Nina doesn't get to see much of him these days, you know, as they are dating. Poor lady, she keeps on waiting each day to see him appear, but he is very busy with the murder case.'

'Murder?'

'Yes, that of the French scientist, you know? ... it has been in all the news.'

'Oh yes! How sad. I knew her in fact ...sorry I didn't introduce myself, I am Professor Jonas'

'Oh, nice to meet you Professor, and I am Ah Cheew, the owner of this restaurant.'

'Well, that's nice to meet you indeed. I have to say that my food was utterly delicious, thank you. You will see more of me, I promise.'

'Am glad that you liked the vindaye, Nina

makes them fresh you know, please do come. It will be a pleasure to see you next time.'

Jonas left after bidding goodbye to Ah Cheew leaving a tip for Nina. Ah Cheew was sure to inch more to extracting some information from this man next time she sees him. He seems to be more manageable than the Frenchman.

An air of classical mandarin music started to play. That was a signal from Nina that she should return to her place and count the earnings from lunchtime. Money and gossip make Ah Cheew very happy indeed.

*

« On an island of the Dodo, there lived a young woman called Floralie. She was the only daughter of a fisherman and his wife;

respectable folk of the islands, whose only ambition was to see their daughter happily married. But, in spite of her beauty, Floralie had never fallen in love; and as she was headstrong, demanding and proud, the young men of the island soon found their solace elsewhere.

Her mother said: "Beware of your pride. Young men are not so plentiful that you can afford to turn them away. If you are not spoken for by your twenty-fifth birthday; an old maid you shall be, left on the shelf, and then what shall become of us?"

But Floralie was undeterred.

She said: "The men of the islands are rough and uncouth. Their hands are rough; their faces sour. I shall catch myself a prince, and bear a handsome princeling, and all the girls of the island shall envy my good fortune."

The mother said sharply: "What do you mean?"

Floralie only shook her hair, which was dark as ebony with bleached ends which lit up as fiery as the sunset, and said: "I shall have my princeling within the year, you wait and see." And nothing more could her mother get from her, however much she tried.

Now Floralie had a grandmother living on the mainland, whose knowledge of the ocean was greater than that of anyone around. A widow of many years, and wise, she knew all the old tales and legends, and had passed them on to her granddaughter almost as soon as the child could talk. Tales of Krishna, tales of Daïnes and spirits that inhabit crossroads and the long tresses of banyan trees. Tales of the monsters that come up from the darkest depths to die; tales of the traveling folk of the woods, who can walk in the skins of animals, tales of formidable shape shifters.

"Once, we all lived in the sea," the grandmother had told her. "Its salt runs in our blood; our tears are memories of the ocean."

"Then why did we leave it?" Floralie had asked.

"Because we were fools," came the reply. "We wanted to conquer. We forgot the voice of the sea, and learned to walk upright on land, and to pretend we were better than animals."

17

Baptiste

Baptiste often went out as early as possible, trying to beat the other fishermen to a good catch of king fish, *kato* and red snapper. Those which fetched high prices at the quayside. He would head to the jagged rocks one mile or so off Baie du Tombeau, taking with him his usual accoutrements to keep him company while he put his lines out – a pack of the finest local ganja and his guitar. He didn't play it too well, it was an old beat-up thing his cousin Jaz, had given him. He would drop anchor near those rocks, lash the rudder, light his spliff and strum to himself while the white, neon disc of the sun appeared on the horizon, pushing itself up, rising slowly, omnipotent into the silver-blue sky.

Baptiste was strumming his guitar and singing to himself when she first raised her barnacled, seaweed-encrusted head from the flat, emerald sea, its stark hues of turquoise, not yet stirred. Plainly, the mermaid popped up and watched him for some

time before he glanced around and caught sight of her.

'*Bon Dié Mama! ki été sa!*' he exclaimed, blinking his eyes in utter bewilderment.

She ducked back under the water. He

quickly put down his guitar and peered hard into the water. It wasn't fully daylight yet. He rubbed his eyes, as if to make them see better.

'Eh la!' he called across the water.

'*Dou dou*. Come. *Mami vini*! Come...Come.'

He put one hand on his heart because it felt was leaping around inside his chest. His limbs were shaking in fear and excitement because he knew what he'd seen. A woman from the depths.

Right there, in the water. An iridescent-skinned woman, not black, not African.

Not yellow, not a Chinese woman, or a woman with golden hair from la France. Rather the hues of blue green like a *kato* fish yet blinding silver. He had seen her shoulders, her head, her pert breasts, and her long black hair like ropes, all hooked up with sea anemones and algae… he thinks he also saw barnacles. A mermaid? He stared at the spot of her appearance for some time. He took a good look at his spliff; was it something really strong, some Afghani mix he smoked that morning? He shook himself and gazed hard at the sea, waiting for her to pop back up.

'Come back,' he shouted into the deep blueness of the sea. The mermaid had held her head up high above the waves, and he'd seen a certain expression on her face, like she'd been studying him. He waited.

Nothing happened. Not that day.

He sat down in his pirogue and, for some reason, tears fell for his mother, just like that. For Marie Ange, his good mother, the *boulette* dim sum maker of the village, who died two years ago. He had never felt such strong emotions for any other woman.

Later, when he racked his brain, he thought of all those stories he'd heard since childhood, tales of half and half sea creatures, except those stories were of mermen. Coquille d'Argent legend told of mermen who lived deep in the sea and came onto land now to mate with river maidens – old time stories, from the colonial era.

All considered as myths to enchant kids around the campfire when night fell and their parents were too tired to look after them, the old folks then took over weaving stories so the younger ones could sleep with wild images in their heads. It was the only way to keep their attention away from the bleakness of their situations in the sugar plantation camps. The tradition carried on in post-colonial times, even after independence from the British. The older fishermen liked to talk in the *boutik* on the foreshore, open sometimes late into the night, after a fair bit of rum had been shared and fried *Corne* fish had been eaten as *gajak*.

The mermen of Coquille d'Argent were just that: local fables. It was November, time of the mackerel migration south to the waters of Baie du Tombeau, the time of the dry season, of fruit trees exploding in the hills, bright yellow and orange laden with fruit, like bombs of sulphur. The time when the ubiquitous flame tree begins to bloom in its exuberant carmine clusters. From that moment, when that red-skinned woman rose and disappeared as if to tease him.

Baptiste ached to see her again. He felt a bittersweet melancholy, a soft caress to his spirit. Nothing to do with what he'd been smoking. That day, a part of him lit up, a part he'd no idea was there to kindle. He had felt a sharp stabbing sensation, right there in the flat part between his ribs, in his solar plexus.

'Come back …,' he said, soft and gentleman like, under the scorching sun till the sweat of his face was tight with salt. Something had happened. She had risen from the waves, chosen him, a humble fisherman.

'*Viens, mo zoli fi,*' he pleaded, this time softer still, as if to lure her, but the water had settled back flat.

The horizon seemed its usual linear recess where the eyes couldn't see anymore. Baptiste knew that underneath his boat was a vast world with creatures of unthinkable diversity. He just wanted one of them. One of his visions. Time would have to kneel and offer him an extended opportunity.

The next morning, Baptiste went again to the exact same spot by those jagged rocks and waited for several hours, but saw or heard nothing. He smoked nothing either, in case it blurred his vision. Next day, the same thing happened. For four days he went out to those rocks in his pirogue. He would cut the engine, throw out the anchor, and wait. He told no one what he had seen. He avoided the *boutik*, which was the village's gossip hub.

He avoided his cousins in Arsenal. He went home to his small shack, one he'd built himself with a blue tin roof surrounded by banana trees, where he lived with Boule, his cross-breed dog.

He went to bed as soon as night fell so as to get up in the early hours. He needed to see the creature he had seen again, to believe his eyes. He needed to cool what had become a blaze in his heart, to pacify the buzz that had started in his brain. He had never felt like this before, certainly not for any woman. He had had lovers before but they all stayed briefly and went their ways. This time was different. He was spellbound by this creature. His waiting each day was gnawing his patience to the bone. He had no choice but to wait for another night to pass by.

Then, around day five, by six o'clock while the sun spread its golden rays on the shimmering water, while he was strumming his guitar, humming a song, she appeared! This time she splashed the water with one hand and made a squeaky sound. Baptiste froze, his heart beating fast, but he stayed still and watched her.

This time believing his own eyes. It was real.

The creature was floating close to the side of his boat. She had long black hair and large, shining eyes, and was giving him a long-fixed stare.

She cocked her head, and it was only then Baptiste realized she was watching his guitar. Slowly, so as not to frighten her, he picked it up and began to strum and hum a tune, softly. She stayed there, floating, watching him, stroking the water, slowly, with her arms and her massive tail.

Each time she moved, the scales on her body shimmered and caught the sunlight to shine like myriads of tiny diamonds, transmitting rainbow prismed rays. With her head and shoulders up out of the water, Baptiste could get a better look at her. Everything about her was beautiful. From her silver hair, to her shimmery skin and eyes that shone like pure gold. Her slender body was adorned with all sorts of trinkets and jewellery. Pearls, shells and precious stones. These were all unfamiliar sights on one of her kind. As far as Baptiste knew, no one on the island had ever seen a mermaid before. She looked mesmerized by his humming and the sounds of the guitar. As if proving that music makes magic within every creature on earth, including mermaids. More like the music of the spheres which even he did not know he could play. She hadn't heard music for a long time, maybe a thousand years, and she was gripped in a mysterious way to this human.

That morning, Baptiste played her soft hymns he'd learnt as a boy, from his father. He sang holy songs for her, songs which brought tears to his own eyes, and there they both stayed, on this second meeting closer than anyone could have wished. She stayed afloat moving slowly around the pirogue.

Then, in one flash, she dived and disappeared into the depths. Baptiste felt like the enchantment was broken. He kept on going to the same spot, waiting for hours, strumming his guitar. She never appeared again.

Some days, Baptiste wandered to the *boutik*, he found that some men spoke hard and loud hurting his ears. He didn't feel as if he any longer belonged to this crowd. His eyes remained transfixed on the ocean. Wishing he could see a familiar shimmer, but there was nothing. He noticed, out of the corner of his intent gaze, Léon who had displayed his early morning's catch onto his flattened *Vacoas tentes*.

'Ki li dire monwar? tou Korek?'

'Oui frère ... Korek, toi ?!' *'Ala li la'* replied Léon showing his catch. Baptiste gave him a

little wave, and glanced at the lifeless fish and felt sick in the stomach. Turquoise flanked parrot fish with their toothy beak-like mouths, *sacré chien* adorned in a pale greyish body, looked very ordinary, but they fetched Léon the best prices. Tiny red rougets shone like little *maison rouz* mangoes with a tail. Baptiste thought of the mermaid and felt a knot in his throat.

What if she gets caught like these cheerless fish?

Léon would indeed be a happy fisherman. Baptiste shivered in dread. He retreated to the giant banyan trees on the shore and sat there, with his eyes welded to the horizon. His life as a fisherman had just changed. He was lost and confused, yet elated. She had chosen him to show herself. He was indeed, incredibly lucky.

18

Mûden

Mûden had swum for miles, further and further away from the palace she'd called home all her life. She had made sure to avoid areas that she knew would be heavily guarded, Mûjik rock especially.

So, instead she found herself traveling east. Nothing about her surroundings looked familiar anymore. But getting lost wasn't a risk she needed to concern herself with. She, like all of her people, possessed an immaculate sense of direction. No matter how many times she'd change course, she always knew in the back of her mind where home was. She'd find her way back with ease. At first, she'd felt anxious, be it for another reason.

Has someone noticed her departure? Would she be intercepted and taken back home, just like all those years ago? After her earlier disagreement with her father, the punishment for her act of rebellion, would be unpleasant to say the least. The General under the Seas of Mû could be harsh when his authority was challenged. He wouldn't let a small detail like Mûden, being his only daughter discourage him from dishing out justice. Even Mûfat, who'd always had a soft spot for his baby sister, wouldn't be able to shield her from that. As time passed, Mûden felt calmer and more self-assured. She had been surreptitious enough to slip away unseen.

For once in her life, she was completely alone. And the views that accompanied her journey were indescribable. Schools of colourful fish darting through exotic coral reefs, as far as the eye could see. The water even smelled different here. Fresher, crisper. She didn't just stay down by the ocean floor either.

In her eagerness to discover as much as she could, she swam closer and closer to the surface, hoping to catch a glimpse of the kind of creatures who lived beyond the sea, but which she had only ever heard of in stories and song. Birds. Red Tailed Tropic bird, Paille-enQueue. Albatrosses. There weren't any out in the open sea, at least not on this day.

Mûden did not let that discourage her. She kept going, until the landscape changed dramatically once again. A huge black basaltic landmass came into view. It grew upwards out of the ocean floor and rose steeply, extending up and out of the water. She had never seen anything as imposing in her life.

"An island," Mûden whispered to herself, as she tried to catch her breath. Having come so close to the Other World, she could not stop herself from exploring further. Sure enough, the winged creatures she had wanted to see earlier were plentiful around the shoreline. She approached the island and made her way up to the surface, mesmerized by the way the birds moved through the skies. Flapping their wings, up and down, diving and soaring effortlessly through the air. It was a most beautiful thing. How were they able to do that without being in the water? She had no idea. Mûden knew she should be careful, although her curiosity spurred her on to explore more and more of this foreign land.

In any case, it seemed like nobody was watching. Until she saw a small boat with a man looking lonely and playing an instrument. The sounds coming from it drew her attention. They resounded in the water, amplifying the notes. She raised her head furthermore to listen.

The man saw her! She wasn't afraid but looked at him too. His skin looked like the dark moray eel on the reefs, he had a gentle face with dark twinkling eyes. He came forward and leaned over the boat, staring at Mûden. She swiftly dunked under the water with only her face submerged. Her skin glistened under the sunlight sending light prisms to sparkle like thousands of micro rainbows. She was unaware what she had sparked into the man's heart, at the sight of her.

The latter was in awe to see a creature so beautiful. Better than in his imagination, when he was a little boy listening to his grandmother's tales of the sea and its mythical creatures, which only fishermen knew in such detail. He drifted back to the sight of such an ethereal face and eased in a slow breath.

Then, within a split of a second, the creature disappeared into the depths. Baptiste felt gutted to the core.

He went around the boat and looked around several times, but the emerald vastness showed him nothing more. He went back ashore, lost in his thoughts about what he had witnessed.

Could he tell anyone in the tavern? No, most of them would be drunk and laugh at him, thinking he had had a bit too much of his rum while waiting for his catch. Baptiste didn't even realize that he did not draw in his nets. The banyan gave him a quizzical look seeing he moored his boat without unloading any catch.

Some days are like that, when all that matters are trying to find where reality ends and myth inhabits.

*

'Friends and colleagues,' Prof Jonas said, slowly scanning the expectant faces. 'We all know why we are here.'

Their attention shifted to the screen at the far end of the room.

'Atlantis! Now, you may be asking yourselves why are we talking of Atlantis while we are standing on an island in the Indian Ocean, well, that's the very reason we are here today.' Jonas breathed. 'I must ask you to be patient.'

Fabio, who arrived early, scanned the faces, unaware how desperate they were to hear Jonas and Prof Katya's translation of the text. The Russian researcher's work was a fresh and valuable addition to the findings that late Prof Valériane Ducasse was working on, under complete secrecy.

'Before I speak, I propose that Dr Svetlanova give us an account of the Atlantis story as we know it. Katya, if you will, please.'

The audience let out a momentary hum, showing their anticipation of discovering a new scientist on the stage.

She was a tall woman, with a short pixie cut in platinum blond hair, and dressed very casually in a white linen dress. Her steely blue eyes spoke all of what the islanders were not familiar with, the Steppes and the Tundra. Human eyes evolved from dark to light blues to accommodate and retain more light, this was an end result of the ice age survivors.

'With pleasure, Professor.' Katya and Jonas had become friends when she was a sabbatical fellow under his guidance at Cambridge. In recent years, they had been together in Athens when the city had been devastated by a massive earthquake, cracking open the Acropolis to reveal a cluster of rock-cut chambers which contained the long-lost archive of the ancient city. Katya and Jonas had assumed responsibility for publishing the texts relating to Greek exploration, beyond the Mediterranean.

Only a few months earlier their faces had been splashed over front pages all round the world following a press conference in which they revealed how an expedition of Greek and Egyptian adventurers had sailed across the Indian Ocean as far as the South China Sea. Katya was also one of the world's leading experts on the legend of Atlantis, and had brought with her copies of the relevant ancient texts. She picked up two small books and opened them at the marked pages.

'Gentlemen, may I first say what a pleasure it is for me to be invited to this symposium. It is a great honour for the Moscow Institute of Palaeography. Long may the spirit of international cooperation continue.'

There was an appreciative murmur from around the table with visible nods. Some were just standing as vigils. They were the journalists. The press was invited to the symposium in the aim of reporting about the scientific discoveries while clearing the air over the dark cloud of mystery over the recent murder. It was a strategy of Fabio, to which Inspector Sanjiv was most amicable to. In fact, he had found the idea brilliant, that the public be fed on some distracting news without losing the thread of the case. It would look like the authorities were fully assuming their responsibilities.

'I will be brief. First, you can forget virtually everything you have ever heard about Atlantis.' Katya spoke with a seemingly light accented English. Her years spent at Cambridge university enabled her to master the East English timbre. She had

assumed a serious scholarly demeanour, the twinkle in her eye gone, both Jonas and Fabio found themselves concentrating entirely on what she had to say.

'You may think Atlantis was a global legend, some distant episode in history half remembered by many different cultures, preserved in myth and legend around the world. Like the stories of the Great Flood,' 'But you would be wrong. There is only one source.' She picked up the two books as she spoke. 'The ancient Greek philosopher Plato.'

The others settled back to listen.

'Plato lived in Athens from 427 to 347 BC, a generation after Herodotus,' she said. 'As a young man Plato would have known of the orator Pericles, would have attended the plays of Euripides and Aeschylus and

Aristophanes, would have seen the great temples being erected on the Acropolis. These were the glory days of classical Greece, the greatest period of civilization ever known.'

Katya put down the books and pressed them open.

'These two books are known as the Timaeus and the Critias. They are imaginary dialogues between men of those names and Socrates, Plato's mentor whose wisdom survives mainly through the writings of his pupil. 'Here, in a fictional conversation, Critias tells Socrates about a mighty civilization, one which came forth out of the Atlantic Ocean nine thousand years before. The Atlanteans were descendants of Poseidon, god of the sea. However, the story goes beyond Atlantis. There was an island beyond the Pillars of Hercules; the *island was larger than Libya and Asia put together. And these two were adjoined to a greater land mass which extended to the unknown East. This continent, home to a great and wonderful empire, had rule over the whole island and several others, over fragments of continents, and, furthermore, the men of Atlantis had subjugated the parts of Libya within the Columns of Hercules as far as Egypt, and of Europe as far as Tyrrhenia.*

Libya was the ancient name for Africa, Tyrrhenia was central Italy and the Pillars of Hercules the Straits of Gibraltar. However, Plato was neither a geographer nor historian, he was a philosopher. His theme was a monumental war between the Athenians and the Atlanteans, one which the Athenians naturally won but only after enduring the most extreme danger.' She looked again at the text. 'Now the climax, the nub of the legend. These final few sentences have tantalized scholars for more than two thousand years, and have led to more dead ends than I can count. Afterwards there occurred violent earthquakes and floods; and in a single day and night of misfortune all your warlike men in a body sank into the earth, and the huge continent, in like manner, disappeared into the depths of the sea.'

Katya closed the book and gazed quizzically at Jonas. 'What would you expect to find on this unknown continent? And what was it called?'

Jonas hesitated uncharacteristically, aware that she would be judging his scholarship for the first time. *'Atlantis has always meant much more than simply a myth, but the other larger continent spanning from East to West, South of the Indian Ocean was called Mû, and all of it is that of a mighty lost civilization,*' he replied.

'*To the ancients, it was a fascination with the fallen, with greatness doomed by arrogance and hubris. Every age has had its Mû or Atlantis fantasy, always harking back to a world of unimagined splendour overshadowing all of history. To the Nazis it was the birthplace of Überman, the original Aryan homeland, spurring a demented search around the world for racially pure descendants. To others it was the Garden of Eden, a Paradise Lost.*' Katya nodded and spoke quietly.

'*If there is any truth to this story, if the relic we bring you today gives us any more clues, then we may be able to solve one of the greatest mysteries of ancient history.*'

There was a pause as the assembled gathering looked from one to the other, anticipation and barely repressed eagerness on their faces. 'Thank you, Katya.' Jonas stood up, obviously more comfortable speaking on his feet. He was an accomplished lecturer, used to commanding the full attention of his audience.

'I suggest the Atlantis story is not history but allegory. Plato's intention was to draw out a series of moral lessons. In the Timaeus, order triumphs over chaos in the formation of the Cosmos. In the Critias, men of self-discipline, moderation and respect for the law triumph over men of pride and presumption. The conflict with Atlantis was contrived to show that Athenians had always been people of resolve who would ultimately be victorious, in any war. Even Plato's pupil Aristotle

thought Atlantis never existed.'

Jonas put his hands on the table and leaned forward. *'I suggest Atlantis is a political fable. Plato's account of how he came by the story is a whimsical fiction like Swift's introduction to Gulliver's Travels, where he gives a source which is plausible, but could never be verified.'*

He was playing devil's advocate, Fabio knew. He always relished the old professor's rhetorical skills, a reflection of years spent in the world's great universities.

'It would be useful if you could run over Plato's source,' Hiebermeyer said. 'Certainly.' Jonas looked at his notes, flipped over them to an impatient audience. *'Critias was Plato's great-grandfather. Critias claims that his own great-grandfather heard the Atlantis story from Solon, the famed Athenian lawmaker. Solon in turn heard it from an aged Egyptian priest at Saïs in the Nile Delta.'*

Jonas did a quick mental calculation.

'Solon lived from about 640 to 560 BC. He would only have been admitted to the temple as a venerated scholar. If we therefore assume, he visited Egypt as an older man, but not too old to travel, that would place the encounter sometime in the early sixth century BC, say 590 or 580 BC.'

'If, that is, we are dealing with fact and not fiction. I would like to pose a question. How is it that such a remarkable story was not known more widely? Herodotus visited Egypt in the middle of the fifth century BC, about half a century before Plato's time. He was an indefatigable researcher, a magpie who scooped up every bit of trivia, and his work survives in its entirety. Yet there is no mention of Atlantis.

Why?' Jonas' gaze ranged around the room taking in each of them in turn. He sat down. After a pause a man in a blue polo shirt and khaki trousers stood up and spoke.

'I think I might be able to answer your question.' He paused briefly. 'In our world we tend to think of historical knowledge as universal property. There are exceptions of course, and we all know history can be manipulated, but in general little of significance can be kept hidden for too long. Well, ancient Egypt was not like that.'

The others listened attentively. *'Unlike Greece and the Near East, whose cultures had been swept away by invasions, Egypt had an unbroken tradition stretching back to the early Bronze Age, to the early dynastic period around 3100 BC. Some believe it stretched back even as far as the arrival of the first agriculturalists almost four thousand years earlier.'* There was a murmur of interest from the others.

'Yet by the time of Solon this ancient knowledge had become increasingly hard to access. It was as if it had been divided into interlocking fragments, like a jigsaw puzzle, then packaged up and parcelled away.'

He paused, pleased with the metaphor. 'It came to reside in many different temples, dedicated to many different gods. The priests came to guard their own parcel of knowledge covetously, as their own treasure. It could only be revealed to outsiders through divine intervention, through some sign from the gods. Oddly,' he added with a twinkle in his eye, 'these signs came most often when the applicant offered a benefaction, usually gold.'

Both Fabio, Professor Jonas and Professor Katya were most intrigued by this unknown intervenant.

'Can someone hand over a microphone to this gentleman please?' Jonas asked the technicians.

'So, you can buy knowledge?' He asked.

'Yes, but only when the circumstances were right, on the right day of the month, outside the many religious festivals, according to a host of other signs and auguries. Unless everything was right, an applicant would be turned away, even if he arrived with a shipload of gold.'

'So, the Atlantis story could have been known in only one temple, and told to only one Greek.'

'Precisely.' The man in the polo shirt nodded solemnly at Jonas.

'Maybe the audience would like to know your name, Sir?'

'I am Pez Moshe.'

'Thank you for your intervention Mr Moshe.'

Pez continued, 'Only a handful of Greeks ever made it into the temple scriptoria. The priests were suspicious of men like Herodotus who

were too inquisitive and indiscriminate, traveling from temple to temple. Herodotus was sometimes fed misinformation, stories that were exaggerated and falsified. He was, as you say, led up the garden path.

'The most precious knowledge was too sacred to be committed to paper. It was passed down by word of mouth, from high priest to high priest.'

I totally agree with you, Katya came forward, '*Most of it died with the last priests when the Greeks shut down the temples. What little made it to paper was lost under the Romans, when the Royal Library of Alexandria was burnt down during the civil war in 48 BC and the Daughter Library went the same way when the Emperor Theodosius ordered the destruction of all remaining pagan temples in AD 391. We already know some of what was lost from references in surviving ancient texts. The Geography of Pytheas the Navigator.*

The History of the World by the Emperor Claudius. The missing volumes of Galen and Celsus. Great works of history and science, compendia of pharmaceutical knowledge that would have advanced medicine immeasurably. We can barely begin to imagine the secret knowledge of the Egyptians that went the same way.'

Pez sat down and Katya spoke again. '*I'd like to propose an alternative hypothesis. I suggest Plato was telling the truth about his source. Yet for some reason Solon did not write down an account of his visit. Was he forbidden from doing so by the priests?'*

She picked up the books and continued. '*I believe Plato took the bare facts he knew and embellished them to suit his purposes. Here I agree in part with Professor Jonas. Plato exaggerated to make Atlantis a more remote and awesome place, fitting for a distant age.*

So, he put the story far back in the past, made Atlantis equal to the largest landmass he could envisage, and placed it in the western ocean beyond the boundaries of the ancient world. We know that there was a much larger continent and mightier race, except that the Greeks were the scholars of the time, and ruled out theories which were undisputed. She looked at Jonas. 'There is a theory about Atlantis, one widely held by archaeologists. We are fortunate in having one of its leading proponents among us today. Dr Jonas?'

The latter was already flicking the remote control to a map of the Aegean with the island of Crete prominently in the centre. *'It only becomes plausible if we scale it down,'* he said. *'If we set it nine hundred rather than nine thousand years before Solon, we arrive at about 1600 BC. That was the period of the great Bronze Age civilizations, the New Kingdom of Egypt, the Canaanites of Syro-Palestine, the Hittites of Anatolia, the Mycenaeans of Greece, the Minoans of Crete. This is the only possible context for the Atlantis story.'*

He aimed a pencil-sized light pointer at the map. 'And I believe the only possible location is Crete.' He looked at Hiebermeyer. 'For most Egyptians at the time of the Pharaohs, Crete was the northerly limit of their experience. From the south it's an imposing land, a long shoreline backed by mountains, yet the Egyptians would have known it was an island from the expeditions they undertook to the palace of Knossos on the north coast.'

'What about the Indian Ocean?' Pez asked. 'You can forget that,' Jonas said.

'In Plato's day the sea to the west of Gibraltar was unknown, a vast ocean leading to the fiery edge of the world. So

that was where Plato relocated Atlantis.

His readers would hardly have been awestruck by an island in the Mediterranean.'

'And the word Atlantis?' *'The sea god Poseidon had a son Atlas, the muscle-bound colossus who carried the sky on his shoulders. The Atlantic Ocean was the Ocean of Atlas, not of Atlantis. The term Atlantic first appears in Herodotus, so it was probably in widespread currency by the time Plato was writing.'*

Jonas paused and looked at the others. *'Before seeing our relic, I would have argued that Plato made up the word Atlantis, a plausible name for a lost continent in the Ocean of Atlas. We know from inscriptions that the Egyptians referred to the Minoans and Mycenaeans as the people of Keftiu,*

 people from the north who came in ships bearing tribute. I would have suggested that Keftiu, not Atlantis, was the name for the lost continent in the original account. Now I'm not so sure.

If this papyrus really does date from before Plato's time then clearly, he didn't invent the word.'

'There may be a hint of this in the legend of Theseus and the Minotaur,' Katya said.

'Theseus the Athenian prince wooed Ariadne, daughter of King Minos of Knossos, but before taking her hand he had to confront the Minotaur in the Labyrinth. The Minotaur was half bull, half man, surely a representation of Minoan strength in arms.'

Pez joined in. '*The Greek Bronze Age was rediscovered by men who believed that the legends did contain a kernel of truth. Sir Arthur Evans at Knossos, Heinrich Schliemann at Troy and Mycenae. Both believed the Trojan wars of Homer's Iliad and Odyssey, written down in the eighth century BC, preserved a memory of the tumultuous events which led to the collapse of Bronze Age civilization.*' '*That brings me to my final point,*' Jonas said.

'*Plato would have known nothing of Bronze Age Crete, which had been forgotten in the Dark Age that preceded the classical period. Yet there is much in the story reminiscent of the Minoans, details Plato could never have known. But why wasn't Mû accounted for nor written about?*' '*Atlantis was very lofty and precipitous on the side of the sea, and encompassed a large mountain and plain.'*

Just as the Minoans were excellent hydraulic engineers, so the Atlanteans made cisterns, some open to the heavens, others roofed over, to use in winters as warm baths. There were the baths for the kings and for private persons and for horses and cattle. And then the bull.'

Jonas pressed the selector and another view of Knossos appeared, this time showing a magnificent bull's horn sculpture beside the courtyard. He read again.

'There were bulls who had the range of the temple of Poseidon. The kings, being left alone in the temple, after they had offered prayers to the god that they might capture the victim which was acceptable to him, hunted the bulls, without weapons, but with staves and nooses.'

Jonas turned towards the screen and flicked through the remaining images.

'A wall painting from Knossos of a bull with a leaping acrobat. A stone libation vase in the shape of a bull's head. A golden cup impressed with a bull-hunting scene. An excavated pit containing hundreds of bulls' horns, recently discovered below the main courtyard of the palace.'

'Are you ready?' Jonas asked the audience. There was a fervent murmur of assent. The atmosphere in the room tightened perceptibly.

He reached down and unlocked his briefcase, dimmed the main lights and switched on a fluorescent lamp over a shining object resting on a plate. There was a murmur from the audience, some getting up from their chairs to take a better look, moving forward, annoying those in the way.

'Do you know what this is?!'

Jonas pointed to a man with a white shirt sitting quietly in the front row. He briefly smiled and looked around the audience acquiescing the indication from Jonas politely.

'Mr Ducasse, the husband of my late associate and friend Professor Valériane Ducasse graciously brought us this - the relic we all are baffled to discover. Or rather, what she discovered. This is the very reason that we are here and having bored you with so much of ancient history. This is the 'proof' that the tiny island of Mauritius is not an island ....!'

This garnered an exclamative reaction from the audience, which broke the attentive silence. Jonas cleared his throat and asked for everybody's attention again.

'Yes, this is a breakthrough in the unwritten annals of paleo history, we have proof of the existence of another species which preclude that of us humans, of a race before any other, far more sophisticated and advanced that we could possibly have imagined. In our regressive minds, we would call them aliens, had they come from space, yet they are from our planet!

They belonged to this very land. Mauritius. The land of Mû which has been recorded only by the Thamizen, or the Tamils as we know them today. Some know this continent as Kumari Kandam. All of this takes a new turn by the formidable discovery of the late Professor Ducasse. She found this!' To which Jonas held high the plate containing the object.

'What does this look like to you?' The press until now, quiet and taking notes, started flashing their cameras and shooting pictures in a row. Jonas held his hand high and asked them to stop.

'This is not a gem?'

'Ahhhh...ohhh!' The audience responded unanimously.

'This is a piece of skin of a race which now lives under water. They have evolved to be able to do so. And Professor Ducasse discovered that they came ashore here ... yes right here on the shores of the island' Someone raised an arm, Jonas allowed the question, although it wasn't question time.

'How can you be sure? It's from Mauritius?'

'Because it's their land, their continent-Mû. They never left. The island sits on a vast continental shelf which was part of Mû, submerged millions of years ago. Yes, humans didn't evolve from the apes in Africa as we know, there were others much more ancient that we can believe.'

Pez stood up, asking to speak. He was given a microphone.

'Professor, you realise what you are saying? That's gurgling down the whole history of humankind, that's giving Darwin a tight slap.'

'No, Jonas pleaded, that's not what I am saying. Evolution has taken place, and Charles Darwin remains the forefather in writing about evolution stemming from his observations from pigeons and others. However, our Earth has been constantly evolving also. Many periods of natural catastrophes and disasters. The continents drifted for sure and continue to do so. Just as are the gradual submersions of smaller islands.

The oceans are reclaiming land masses. This is how the planet evolves through each age, naturally or precipitated by man's destructive actions upon the environment. The continent of Mû has existed.

Sadly, we have come to the end of this session. We shall resume after lunch. Thank you for your presence and attention. Bon Appétit!'

Jonas switched off the screen behind him, and was surrounded by a huge round of applause from the audience. Katya got up from her chair and joined Jonas in the room at the back of the stage. The audience dispersed to the lunch buffet spread out on neatly arranged tables with ruffle pleated tablecloths. Usually a great mix of local dishes with continental choices reward such events. Fabio took leave after gulping in two glasses of chilled tamarind juice.

*

Inspector Sanjiv got a call from Fabio who decided to pick him up discreetly for a short drive towards Baie du Tombeau. After leaving the congested roads of the city centre, and braving a few irritated bursts at some raucous drivers in the haste to reach home, the duo arrived past the new roundabouts in the districts.

The Inspector's mood improved as he mounted the off-road lane in the sturdy 4x4 police vehicle. It was the quickest way to cover the island's mixed terrain and the best perk of his job, even though it sometimes took him three attempts to start the engine.

They arrived at a leafy gardened villa while the trade winds had stopped blowing, breathless heat surrounding them in a sticky humidity. The nearby police station lies in a section of the island that few holidaymakers visit. Most simply check into their villas and remain there, only emerging for cocktails at Chan's Bar, or pick a take away at Briani house, before jetting home.

Sanjiv scans the dense thickets that lie beyond the stone-paved path. The island has changed a great deal since his childhood, but the developers have retained the illusion of a tropical jungle, even though almost a hundred villas lie hidden among the trees. When he was a boy, turtles still crawled onto the beaches to lay their eggs, and grey giant tortoises roamed the jungles. The island's wildlife still includes plenty of birds but with each new dwelling built as a holiday home, natural habitats are being destroyed without anyone batting an eyelid. Money does not talk -it swears!

A yellow-tailed serin cardinal flies overhead as it flies over its natural surroundings of Tombeau Bay, where a few holidaymakers are taking a dip, their beach towels the only spots of colour on the pale white sand.

Fabio cannot help but exclaim how beautiful the shore line looks with its shimmering turquoise expanse.

 The two men's curiosity rises as they park outside the villa. It looks more like a fairy-tale palace than a villa, with huge terraces built into the side of the hill. It's one of the most impressive properties in this corner of the bay, which isn't surprising. Most houses nearby are fishermen houses, mostly shacks and grounded in their simplicity. The playground for the children is some cleared space which acts as a football pitch on the beach. Everywhere took the shade of the beaten terracotta coloured soil, a characteristic of this region of the island. It then drifts into a dark shade of brown in the north.

The volcanic nature of the island has allowed the chemistry of the earth's crust and mantle to provide many coloured soils around the country, while there is a concentration in one spot called Chamarel. There, seven coloured earths undulate into soft hillocks as a spectacle to the naked eyes of mesmerized tourists and locals alike.

Fabio reassessed the surroundings looking for that particular sign of lavishness which can show some hidden fortune being splurged around. He finds none. So far, his own theory that there might be a particular form of foul play remains his own. He had not even vented it to Inspector Sanjiv. He told him that he wanted to do a discreet re-inspection of the villa of late Professor Ducasse.

Inspector Sanjiv sees his neighbour sweeping the patio. He's known the middle-aged woman all his life, yet suddenly she's unwilling to meet his eye. It's not the first time his police badge has drawn a cool reception.

When he asks if the owner is at home, she tells him to speak to the housekeeper.

'She's in the kitchen now.'

The cleaner shoos him inside with a wave of her hand, returning to her job of sweeping invisible dust from the basaltic ground before he's even said goodbye. The simple elegance of the place increases with each step. The sitting room is bigger than his entire home, and even though the views from his back porch are just as good, they look better framed by perfectly designed French windows. There's an infinity pool with tiles that mirror the bleached-out sky, strings of fairy lights hung between palm trees, and a confetti of bougainvillea petals on the lawn. Michel Ducasse is not home, so the two men come out after meeting the housekeeper who was busy in the kitchen. She allowed them only to have a quick scan of the interiors while she tagged closely behind.

They thank her, before saying goodbye. Something about the property unsettles Fabio as he climbs down the steps of the terrace. It feels ghostly, even though the interior sparkles with light. The place is sterile too, every inch of the floor buffed to a high shine. The bedrooms are all decorated with modern furniture, just a few antiques thrown in, to give the place style. Fabio's curiosity peaks as he notices a leaflet on the coffee table. It carries information about Valériane Ducasse's Reef Revival project, which made it to the media some time ago. It created a bit of disagreement when spread in the news. Local fishermen cooperatives have been trying not to damage the coral reefs for years, but it's a losing battle.

Soon, there will be no breeding grounds for the much sought-after snappers, lobsters and crayfish that appear in every restaurant of the local five-star hotels. If the coral dies, their livelihoods will perish too.

Most of them were grateful that the young scientist had drawn attention to it with the authorities and was putting her energy behind a good cause. Inspector Sanjiv had nonchalantly drawn back the mosquito net around the bed when Fabio spotted something odd. A large piece of coral rested on the bed, a foot wide, scattering sand across the sheets. It was pure white, and felt brittle in his hand, delicate tendrils starting to fragment. Its saline smell was completely distinct.

Why would Valériane Ducasse dirty her sheets with sand-encrusted coral? She could have left it on her dressing table instead. Fabio turned around to look inquisitively at the housekeeper who had crept behind the two men as a shadowy spectre; the latter shrugged her shoulders in response.

Inspector Sanjiv's head is so crammed with questions on leaving, he forgot to say goodbye to the cleaner who was still sweeping the terrace, but she notices it. A stream of Creole curses followed him as he walked away. Fabio had been quietly jotting down notes every now and then. Inspector Sanjiv felt a bit on edge not to be told about his observations.

'Shall we grab some lunch then?' Asks Fabio.

'Yes, why not?'

'The usual joint?', 'Yes, fine by me.'

Inspector Sanjiv nodded affirmatively, thinking he might see Nina at the same time. The thought brought a smile to his heart. They arrived at the eatery with its packed lunch crowd. Nina noticed Inspector Sanjiv and Fabio and immediately came to them.

'Bonjour! Lunch?'

'Bonjour Nina, yes for two, please.'

'Wonton soup, Chicken Moonfan, and the

usual fare...any drinks?'

'A beer for me' said Fabio, looking at Inspector Sanjiv.

'Coke and water please, thank you Nina'.

'What is Moon Fan?' Asked Fabio.

'It's a kind of Chinese rice dish with shiitake mushrooms, prawns, sausage, chicken, it's quite nice. Here, they call it the Chinese briani.'

'Oh! Briani ... I like briani. I will have that then. Thank you.'

'No.... It's not briani, it's quite different.'

'Even better then. And you, what are you having?'

'Maybe stir-fried noodles, something simple.'

The young woman swiftly disappeared into the kitchen. Inspector Sanjiv was burning with curiosity, like popcorn jumping in a well buttered pot. He looked across to Fabio and wondered how to ask the first question.

'So, are you happy with the visit? Anything you have found in particular? What you noted down ...' he realized that the questions tumbled down all at once.

Fabio looked in the emptiness, like lost in his own thoughts before waking up and looking straight at Inspector Sanjiv.

'Am not sure, but there's something that correlates to what Professor Jonas told me.'

'Oh ...yeah, and what's that?'

Nina came back to their table to take the orders. Inspector Sanjiv noticed that she was wearing some gloss on her lips. He liked that discreet attention to his presence.

'So, gentlemen, are you ready? What can I get you?'

'Moonfan for me please, thank you and bring me one of those garlic sauces, it's delicious.'

Nina smiled at Fabio and noted down his order mentally, then shifted her look at Sanjiv. The latter blushed gently.

'For me, *mine frit poulet*, thank you.'

Sanjiv waited for the young woman to be out of sight before giving another attentive glance at Fabio. Almost a puppy look. He wanted to know more about what the French detective had been holding back from him. Since, on his side, he had not made any progress on the murder case.

'It's a matter of money. More money than you and I can imagine!'

'Money? Contraband? Drugs?!'

'No, something unique. You see according to Prof Jonas the sea around us is full of ... diamonds. An insane amount.'

Sanjiv almost choked on his Coca Cola, 'What?! diamonds?' we don't have any deposits or mines as far as I remember from my geography class in school.'

'No, you see I noticed the coral on the bed, and the pamphlet of the protection of the environment. Prof Valériane was also working on a secret discovery. Her killer must be someone from inside who had this confidential information.'

'Her husband surely knew about it, many times the first suspect is the spouse.'

'But not in this case, Mr Ducasse was not aware of the discovery of his wife, yet the lab of Valériane had all the details. Prof Jonas told me he received more information regarding the works in the lab from the consortium of other scientists involved in the project. Do you remember Prof Katya and her exposé? Well, that's what should lead us to some track.'

Sanjiv thought hard about Prof Katya's speech, he was dozing most of the time. He was too ashamed to divulge this shortcoming of his to

 Fabio. So, he stayed quiet. They were thankfully interrupted by Nina who brought in their food on a large platter.

'Here you go.... bon appétit!'.

Both men dived into their meals, quietly, but

with forced attention. Fabio was asking himself how he could make the Inspector understand what they were dealing with, far too risky and complex to understand. Besides lacking in credulity. Inspector Sanjiv was far too drunk on the emptiness of his mind to join pieces to a lead. So, he kept on twirling his *mazavaroo* dunked noodles in an invisible hope to fire his mind.

Ah Cheew in the meantime, had not left the two men from her sight. The horizontal slit of her eyes buried much of her gaze enhanced by her buccal fat. Both Fabio and Inspector Sanjiv couldn't see her watching each of their movements and trying to read their lips whenever they talked. Her efforts to feed the inspector had not reaped what she was expecting, as reward.

Neither did her cajoling to get Nina close to him. She was wiping a peal of sweat off her forehead each time she saw them, both being so indolent of her strenuous inputs to purge out what was going on with first-hand information. Now this French man! Sat there and talking to the inspector in a low voice slurping all her good food. She was dying to get at least one tiny nugget of what they spoke so she could quench her curiosity. She looked up at the clock.

'I had better get out there and finish preparing the dining room. The Mah-jong Matrons like to come in for their rice porridge first thing in the morning. At least one thing in our day will be normal.'

Nina followed her with her eyes from where she stood, tending to the straggling customers.

Lunchtime would be over soon. Inspector Sanjiv and the white man were also leaving.

Soon the cafe would be only a jumble of noises from pots and plates being cleaned.

Marie the helper was here already changing into her work clothes to attack the dishes. Then, it would all be quiet. A time of the day that Nina looked forward to, daily, to recollect her thoughts and stretch her aching back. Ah Cheew wouldn't be back for another hour, Nina was in control of everything ... everything! She loved that thought. It made her smile.

Today, she was going to put some order into her emotions and assess the Inspector Sanjiv dimension in her life. She eyed Ah Cheew's prized possession of Chinese herbal teas in the tin canisters next to her desk. Nina would sneak one tea bag into her cup instead of her daily vanilla Corson.

Ah Cheew said that the Chinese brew had

the power to make one reflect deeply and bring inner peace to the soul. That's what she needed today.

*

The wind was a fierce creature today, fiercer than she had known, since they had come to Bay du Tombeau. The street with the butcher's shop sloped down to the water, and the houses flanking her path sloped likewise. The wind blew the cloying smell of meat away and coated her with fish instead. That was a much better smell.

When Valériane Ducasse had first come to this part of the suburbia, the air had tasted of so much fish that she couldn't think how it would be to live here and swallow it every day. Now she was doing it, and found she got to like it. The fresh *carangues*, *kato*, *sacréchiens*, mullets and mackerels were the daily outgivings of the ocean to the local fishermen. These ancient laid off stevedores had taken to fishing to support their families with a meagre earning each day. At least they could eat, even if not guaranteed a sale.

Valériane Ducasse walked to a hidden corner, the harbour came into sight. It was two walls that made it, and they didn't quite meet, one set a little back from the other. Almost touching, as if reaching, but that gap between.

She turned away from them.

Walked on alone.

The Russian had asked her to work with him for she would be generously rewarded. She was attracted to this man for unknown reasons.

Maybe it was boredom from a life on a tiny

island devoted mainly to her research work. Her husband and herself shared a tacit companionship which manifested itself at some months of the year when he would come down from the metropole.

The tall rugged Russian with steely blue eyes which reminded her of the cold Tundra gave her attention, took her to lavish quiet discreet dinners, and was a good listener. However, there were some areas of his life she did not know, nor was keen to know. They were dark and strange, rooted deep in the earth, where by rights, they should remain. There were devils and unquiet souls. There were insane amounts of money that he talked about and those he kept quiet while exhaling smoke from a cigarette. All this kindled an excitement in the young scientist.

Until this evening, she had not spoken about

her discovery to him. He had given her a long-quizzical look but kept puffing circles of smoke out of his musky Russian cigarettes. Her theory had yet to be proven true. Until then, the Russian gave her shelter in his strong arms. She was contented with this little break.

*

Valériane scrambled up the path and reached a cliff point. The wind grew fiercer the higher she climbed the volcanic rocks while she pushed into it to drive out the devil that plagued her. Up up up, ...walking into the clouds. Her hair got free of its knot and streamed around her so she could not see where to put her feet, but the path guided her.

A crash of the waves talking louder and she saw that she'd come to the top of the cliff and the sea was a way away below, surging a white fury that was like the inside of her head. She pushed aside her hair from her eyes and forced it back into a bun.

And then she saw a woman in the water right below her, in all that mass of swirling foam. She must have fallen from the very spot where she herself now stood. What was she doing here?

How could she fetch help? The waves raged and crashed on the rocks with a frightening roar. She was cursed to watch her die. For what unkindness it was to leave a person in distress without being able to rescue her? She couldn't look away. The body did not disappear and she didn't go under. Her head and her arms stayed clear above, and she moved with the waves rather than fight them. She was swimming!

Valériane could tell she was a woman from that distance by her long yellow hair that trailed behind her, and by her breasts, which were bare. What would the fishermen make of such a catch if they should pull up their nets and find her inside? They would be lucky souls, that I did know, for she was a beautiful creature. Now that she didn't fear she was drowning she could watch her in peace, and just admire the way she spread her hands and carved the water, how her skin gleamed, how she pushed herself forward effortlessly.

She wondered if she was seeing something from her imagination. She had lifted her eyes to heaven and wondered if there was any light through the clouds to enable her to see better in an effort to rescue her, if necessary.

The wind gusted and Valéraine stumbled

forward, leaving the path to get closer to the edge of the cliff, and as she righted herself there was a voice, a call. The wind drowned it, or at least snatched the words away. The wind was the call and the call were in the sea, with the woman. A burst of it again, and she wanted to hear more so she stepped forward, into the wind and the words that spun around her. She closed her eyes and tried to listen. It was just there, and not there, and there again. Another step, then one more. Her feet slid out from under her and she fell heavily against one of the rocks that lay between the path and the cliff edge, and all at once she came to her senses and thought of herself.

She crawled back to the safety of the path. When she looked again, the woman had disappeared. She heard a faint voice again. She scrutinized the crests of the waves.

The world was so full of magic then that Mûden didn't always know when she was awake and when she was asleep and dreaming. At night she'd lean out to the surface to see the sleeping island lit by stars. She'd watch the silvery flicker of distant worlds catching the moon on their wings. She'd smell the coppery, sweet-rot scent of the enchantments she knew lurked under the earth.

She'd hear the steady breathing of the sea, slow and deep as a giant mother. She knew that if she could stretch up over the treetops, she'd see dozens of jellyfish glistening on the stones. She knew that behind her and beneath her was

home, in the warm water that surrounded her lithe body. She saw the woman on the cliff, watching her. She was sure that she saw her!

She tried to think: not about what she had to do, move or stay, but about something bigger than that. Something noble and dramatic, but she couldn't grasp hold of a single thought. Her mind was loud and white and chaotic, she was drawn to the extreme. What her parents always warned her not to do - meet the humans.

The woman watching her now had been coming regularly at the same time every night. Each time, Mûden hid when she saw her, but not today. She wanted to see the human from close up.

So, she swam towards her. When she reached the shallows, she stood herself vertical in the water, scrutinizing in the dark trying to figure out the human. The latter was still, sitting and no moon light fell on her to enable Mûden to decipher her face. She had feet, a permanent trait that humans evolved from their fish derivation.

Valériane blinked her eyes once again. She was sure she saw the same apparition in the water like the previous days. Suddenly, the moonlight caught a fluorescent sparkle from the surface. Like two cat's eyes. Then, what happened almost made her heart explode in her rib cage. The creature came closer and walked out of the crashing wavelets.

She was a mermaid!

Soon her large tail became transparent like washed jellyfish on the shore. Two feet appeared and took a soft sliding 'walk' on the wet sand. A tall woman appeared in all her nakedness.

Mûden took small and steady steps, letting the water creep up her calves until she began to feel grounded when her tail disappeared, the coarseness of the sand tickling her feet. A feeling she only had when she became almost human. She stopped there in the shallows, the water licking her legs.

The moonlight turned her shells, clams, and the sea stones embedded on her body into a dazzling shimmering sight. Valéraine couldn't peel her eyes from her. She had never seen someone some sculpturally tall and beautiful. The woman came closer to her. Valériane didn't want to scare her and extended her hand gently towards her.

The creature smelled of the sea. She responded by blinking her eyes, which shone like prisms.

Valériane remembered having read a recent publication of such eyes.

"Prawn larvae hide from predators by

camouflaging their dark eyes with a light-manipulating material that reflects the colour of the surrounding water.

Some sea creatures, like jellyfish, glass squid and ghost fish, have transparent bodies to avoid being spotted by predators. However, one thing they can't hide is their eyes, which contain dark pigments that are essential for vision. What she had in front of her had human eyes ... but yet different.

"Benjamin Palmer at Ben-Gurion University of the Negev in Israel and his colleagues investigated how transparent-bodied larvae of the giant freshwater prawn (Macrobrachium rosenbergii) conceal their dark eyes from predators. They discovered that their eyes are overlaid by photonic glass – a material made up of a disorderly arrangement of spherical particles that have unusual optical

properties. The structures in the larvae's eyes reflect yellow-green light, matching the colour of the murky estuaries in which they live, suggesting it helps to camouflage them. The key thing is that the colour of the reflector is the same from all viewing angles, as this is important to conceal them from predators. The team found that the photonic glass was made of nanospheres of a substance called isoxanthopterin. Using optical and electron microscopy, they saw that these nanospheres could rearrange themselves to produce slightly different shades of yellow and green. This may allow the larvae to move from shallow yellow water to deeper green water while maintaining their disguise."

Prof Valériane made it a point to follow the pattern of the appearance of the creature and one day feigning to be asleep, followed it through half closed eyes to the thickets when it came out from the rocky side of the beach. It vanished each time without leaving a trace. Today was different, it came close to her. She could smell the depths of the sea emanating from her slippery body. She uttered a timid hello garnering all her positive vibes she could muster. She didn't want to frighten it.

'Shrfrracck ...' it replied back.

'What?' The human instinctive query of quizzing came to Valériane. The creature blinked again and turned its head like a pup trying to understand. It then slid back to the ocean in a myriad of phosphorescent lights. The fine wet sand had puddled where it stood for a while. Valériane waited for it to disappear in the water before shining her torch light into the puddle for she saw that there was something shining there. It was silver ... no gold ... not like an oyster shell ...phosphorescent. She scooped the fine wet sand and looked closely, there were shimmering disc like objects. She put them carefully in a plastic bag and took them home to verify them in good light. This night was very fruitful. Never ever in her wildest dream could she have thought to make such a discovery!

*

"Even if human beings were all saints, the government would still be needed to organize them. But since human beings are not all saints, since all of us are sometimes inclined to break common rules and abuse our neighbours, a government is needed to maintain law and order. This remains its basic moral responsibility, even when it acquires other responsibilities for promoting the welfare of its citizens, since without law and order nothing human can flourish – unless you think that the unconstrained power of the warlord is flourishing.

I am not a pacifist. I do think that the maintenance of just law and order sometimes requires physical coercion. The fact that the need for such coercion is regrettable, even lamentable, does not lessen its necessity. As I see it, whether or not a policy that involves killing – or any other policy, for that matter – is morally right or wrong is not determined simply by its effects or consequences.

What decides its moral quality are the motive and intention of the agent, and the proportionality of its means to its ends? Let me explain.

In order to be morally right, a policy must

primarily want or intend something good or valuable. Not infrequently, however, circumstances confront us with a dilemma: we cannot achieve one thing that is valuable without (at least the risk of) causing damage to another thing that is also valuable.

In such a situation, it might be morally right for us to proceed, knowing that we will probably or even certainly damage the latter. Whether such a choice is morally justifiable depends on the valuable quality of our ultimate goal, but not on that alone. It also requires that the means that might or will cause damage are 'proportionate' – that is, best fitted to achieve the valuable goal, while calibrated to risk minimal damage en route.

The pursuit of what is valuable or good is basic to the moral rightness of anything we do, even if it is not sufficient for it. What is good for us is in our genuine interest. Therefore, there is nothing at all wrong with pursuing our own genuine interests – indeed, we have a duty to do so. As with individuals, so with governments. Governments have a responsibility to look after the interests of all their people. As the French political philosopher Yves Simon wrote during the Abyssinia crisis of 1935, 'What should we think, truly, about a government that would leave out of its preoccupations the interests of the nation that it governs?'

This duty is not unlimited, of course. There cannot be a moral obligation to pursue the interests of one's own people by doing an injustice to others. Still, not every pursuit of national interest does involve injustice; so, the fact that national interests are among the motives for a government's policy need not make it immoral. Sometimes individuals and governments can be well motivated to achieve an important objective, and they can choose their means of getting there conscientiously, and yet, through the bad fortune of relentlessly adverse circumstances, they can still fail. Not all failure to do good or avoid evil is immoral and culpable. Some of it is honest and tragic. Where that is so, the fitting response is not blame, but compassion. History contains an ocean of injustice, most of it unsolved and ignored and now lying beyond correction in this world.

Even with respect to recent crimes, the attempt at human justice is haphazard and its achievement fragmentary. Those sober facts oblige realism. Yet human beings seem to have a deep instinct for justice that will not let us settle for less, obliges us to hope against hope and drives us to our knees. The resultant posture, situated between cynicism and utopianism, is well captured by Reinhold Niebuhr's famous prayer: 'God give us grace to accept with serenity the things that cannot be changed, courage to change the things that should be changed, and the wisdom to distinguish the one from the other.'

Fabio was enjoying his brain chatter while sipping a thick and sweet mango juice at Ah Cheew's joint. There was a lot going on. He liked this kind of moment by himself. Sieving through his thoughts, bickering at his own arguments sometimes brings an illumination.

Nina kept glancing in his direction, waiting for inspector Sanjiv to arrive, but the French man remained seated on his own, sipping his fresh juice and jotting down some notes.

With an empty gaze, seeming to be thinking hard in a flick of a moment, a furrow appearing on his forehead.

Ah Cheew had not left him from the corner of her eyes. Her constant greeting and smile to customers made them into narrow slits but she could see clearly what was happening around her. That French customer had often been seen with Inspector Sanjiv, and the latter had been as tight lipped as a carp since their joint appearances.

Ah Cheew wasn't happy. All her buttering and feeding him were of no avail. She had not moved an inch on the murder case. No further information. She will soon turn into a jade lion in her cage. Immovable and stunted in time. Nina hasn't been doing her part also. Silly woman, all she was interested in was whether the man came and gave her amorous glances.

That's it. Ah Cheew decided she had to find another pawn in her mental game. Just then, Tega came in with a loud round of greeting. He had been missing from the scene for a while. He came closer to the counter and gave a Colgate smile to Ah Cheew. The latter felt a bit dull with her own yellowing teeth.

Well, 'Tega doesn't eat so much of *la sauce Siow* like me', the thought reassured her and she greeted Tega back.

After a few exchanges of how his *Ammay* was doing, politics and what's on the day's menu, Tega went to sit in his regular spot. Fabio got up and left, leaving some money on the table.

He drove over to the highest point of Baie du

Tombeau and looked over the serene spread of the ocean with seamless harmony with the sky. He squinted to look at the horizon and thought of Jonas.

*

'All the answers lay up there to those who could see', he thought aloud. Without knowledge of the sky, no one would know where to find a safe port, when to sail hard and when to seek anchor. The sea

gave the inhabitants of the coast prayers to the stars and the tides, just as a creature from the depth may have done every night when the undersea currents came to a calm. They deserved worship for being the only reliable things in the world. Except, perhaps, for one another. Fabio decided he needed to share his investigation to Prof Jonas before he proceeded to issue an arrest warrant against the culprit. For he now knows for sure who it was! It would be a matter of time before the whole truth came to light.

*

Michel Ducasse twirled around the teaspoon in his cup, his gaze lost to two partridges who were cuddling on the warm soft beaten earth. He knew that his late wife was hiding something from him, but he couldn't put his finger on it.

Far too many hours and years of separation had carved a rift between them. Neither of them made any effort to cross towards the other. They accepted their spaces in their aloofness while enjoying quiet silent moments when they met in their home garden. Now he had to bear with the permanent silence that is hardening day by day.

He last saw Valériane at the small restaurant held by the nosy Chinese lady. He had been there once and found himself observed *sous toutes les coutures* by the owner.

On reflection, when Michel saw his wife that day, he was surprised by the tension between the tall Russian man and herself. As if they had a tacit secret by themselves. Their eyes' locked into each other. He saw Valériane take out something from her bag and stealthily show it to him.

Then, snap it as quickly as she could. Michel understood what it was all about. It all made sense. He stayed a bit longer in the buzzing eatery full of lunch customers, his wife didn't notice him. There were quite a few tourists that day so his white tanned skin didn't attract too much attention.

When he met Valeriane in the early evening to take their habitual *apéro*, both feigned to be their usual self, but the silence was heavier that evening. Valériane seemed preoccupied and he couldn't even pose a question. Such was their understanding. Yet Michel knew that it wasn't the normal wife he had by his side. She had changed. A change he had not noticed and he cursed himself for it.

Beyond the edge of the table, the light dimmed as it passes through the screens before brightening over the dappled trees, the pure blue of the pool, the deep-black shadows of the casuarina trees at the water's edge where the reach of the sun falters late in the day.

Michel pondered more about what he should have done that day, but didn't. What he should have said, but didn't. All that mattered then was his aching heart. Full of distress to perhaps having lost Valériane for good. He never thought someone else could take his place. However, things do happen.

When Michel sipped the last drop of his drink, he came back from his thoughts. He realized that the sun was past its glorious golden orange self and was slowly sinking down to the ocean. He felt a sudden breeze, a slight chill. It always happens despite being on a tropical island. The chill after sunset makes many watchers on the beach wrap up and leave.

Michel got up and went into the house before the mosquitoes made a feast of his legs and arms. He had to look for something in his late wife's office.

19

Macondé

Half an hour along the deserted road, cleaved into the muted red and green mountain rock, the landscape became sparse and rugged. A flurry of silky-haired goats with long mismatched horns skittered across the path. Children ran and skipped around long-bearded nanny goats often commonly called *Jamuna pari*. Roadside geraniums and rockroses gave way to clumps of *fleurs corail* and vast swathes of pink land anemones. Neat rows of mango trees, so iconic of the Mauritian landscape, were replaced by tangle-rooted *la liane lang* that towered precariously overhead anything it laid its grip upon.

Fabio rounded a bend and suddenly, far below in the distance, he saw the sea. The majesty of the scene took his breath away. He wanted to stop but the road, dangerous and unforgiving, had an ornate religious shrine on each hairpin. He guessed many motorists had lost their lives on those sharp corners, by the presence of bunches of flowers... A frightening high rate of road accidents plagued the island for some years now. Mainly due to raucous driving new cars while in the quest of showing off, so the old folks would say.

Fabio stopped by a clearing under a shady huge banyan tree. He lit a cigarette and allowed the stillness of the air around him to bring calm to his stumbling thoughts. He knew one thing – the murderer was much closer home than he thought.

He remembered a fisherman he met in Crete telling him this: "When you spend as much time at the mercy of the sea as I have, your soul forgets how to rest. As a seafarer, your ability to react to the slightest change in the environment, be it internally, in the structure and seaworthiness of your vessel, or externally, in the conditions of the ocean and sky that surround you, means everything. Lives depend on how quickly you can act."

It's exactly why he needed such a long drive to La Prairie, as he found the rock mound strutted into the bay of Macondé always to be the most beautiful spot in Mauritius. It is where he feels completely relaxed. And just now, he needed such a place to come to a halt so he could take the next step. That would be the critical one. This has been his career's most unbelievable and hardest case to crack.

The island's rich and complex culture and folklore didn't help to make it easy to understand for the French detective. Here, fates are conjured over a cut lime and turmeric. Spirits are summoned juxtaposed into baffling African and Indian mixed roots. The island's breath-taking natural beauty reminds one it could be a piece of heaven. Could it have detached itself and fallen?

Fabio couldn't reconcile many of the laid down facts in the Roman way he is used to, he had to bend his ways of thinking and open his mind and understanding. Things are not what they appear to be. Suffering ran deep in the psyche under a shiny smile. The islanders crafted their living in a simplistic manner and told stories which echoed many of life's mysteries. He was to give a tangible, believable denouement of the murder case to the law. That too while grabbing at the powerful barons who ran the show on the political scene. It would be tough! For sure. More likely that he may get his wings clipped if he's not astute enough and quick.

The waves breaking at the rocks down the high spot where he stood created white mist and crests against the clear blue emerald lagoon. Far out, the horizon line remained immutable. Some clouds had gathered over the azure sky, which might a sign of a downpour. Anything is possible. Just like truths on this island. Even the unthinkable can happen. What he was about to reveal would probably be laughed at, many would troll him on social media. Will he be ready to go through all of this to deliver the murderer to justice?

Fabio inflated his lungs with marine air. He felt rejuvenated. Ready for action. He made his way down the mound of Macondé and crossed the road to reach his car.

From there, it was a ride which would be very different from what it was on his way here. He had a new sense of determination.

He could unveil something that would allow the soul of Valériane to rest in peace.

Stars don't cry for me,

Because I sing at night.

Because I hurt my heart,

for the dark-haired girl.

Stars don't tell me off

Because I lament at night.

I'll tell my pain to the stars,

Because they're discreet

Because they have patience

And listen all night,

While I tell them about my pain, and you.

Moon, you've never been

In the mess that I'm in.

And you have the right to ask

What I've become, why I'm unhappy.

But you can't understand,

it's never happened to you.

*

Sunday was a usual day for rest and relaxation. Sacred for islanders who end up by the beach in their eternal festive mood. Any opportunity is good for a picnic on the beach. Inspector Sanjeev was invited to a family lunch at his cousin's place whose wife along with other family members had cooked a feast: chicken biryani, fried fish, fish curry, tuna samosas for *gajak*, cucumber and carrot salad, mixed vegetable pickles.

Sanjeev had tucked in without comment, as if such a meal were an everyday happening. Overeating and swimming do not go hand in hand, however, this is what Mauritians do by the beach. It is a smorgasbord of food and alcohol. Some will venture into the sea for a crawl but would end up floating like a beached whale.

While relaxing under the casuarina trees, Sanjeev received a call from Fabio summoning him to the police station as soon as possible. It was Sunday. Sunday was not, in Sanjeev's book, a day when an Inspector of Police should have to attend to his duties illico presto, that was what junior officers were there for ... That, too, was the natural order of things, yet here he was. On a Sunday. Attending to work duties. Most unnatural. Most unsatisfactory.

His good affable nature took over, and he got up to wash his hands and sped to the station still feeling his stomach far too distended.

He passed by the tiny junction towards the gates of the police station, always open and perpetually lopsided. The rendered boundary walls were grey with large patches of mould, the appearance unimproved despite Sub-Inspector Gaëtan's recent innovation of potted plants set atop. It was like gilding a turd, Sanjeev thought, but he had found no reason to oppose it. No one had stolen any of the pots, which pleased him—it would have been bad for his reputation if they had, and he would have had to do something about it. There was the usual throng of civilians at the gates, much the same as at the hospital across the road. Misfortune and circumstance continued to operate on Sundays. The civilians leapt aside as Sanjeev approached.

A few wished him 'good morning', which he dismissed with a 'humph', again part of the natural order. In his view, power was best expressed in the withholding of common courtesy to those of no consequence. The Inspector responded through to the guard's salute and strode through the doors. The reception desk was unmanned, as were all the other desks in the open-plan office behind. The old dusty ceiling fans spun slowly, redistributing the humid air. His nostrils detected a faint aroma of food. Must be the police mess which stood behind the main building. He was far too full to even think about what was on the Sunday's menu. Probably chicken curry. He entered his office and found Fabio sitting by his desk. The two men greeted each other with a handshake.

'So, what brings you here? Shouldn't you be relaxing by the pool at your hotel on this day?'

'Well, when one is working on a murder case, there's no time to relax, is it?'

Inspector Sanjeev smiled, catching the sarcasm and sat down, all ears and eyes on the French detective. His mind had not left the feast he was attending. And he was eager to know why he was pulled from it with such urgency, while he had not even had the dessert. But he sat stoically and faced Fabio. Someone had brought him a cup of black coffee. Always good mannered the staff were, he felt better.

'We need to issue an arrest warrant'

'Really? Against whom?'

'We have the murderer!' Saying so, Fabio turned his gaze to fix the timber cabinets containing files.

 They were always well kept, and he often wondered how special they were to have such a treatment compared to the grubby metal cabinets.

'*Bon dié*!! Well maybe you could tell me' Inspector Sanjeev was torn between being happy to finally have the murderer and the fact that it wasn't his doing.

Fabio was astute. He grabbed a mint candy from the glass bowl on his office table and started chomping on it as if it was giving him extra energy. A corporal knocked at the door.

'*Oui, entrez*' hailed Inspector Sanjeev. It was to ask if the two men needed any more tea or coffee. Fabio nodded affirmatively, and the corporal left with half a smile.

'So, who is it? A local or foreigner?'

'He is not from here.'

'Aha ... I knew it!' slammed Sanjeev with a fist in the air in a triumphal way. As if, he had contributed to elucidating the mystery.

'First thing in the morning, we make the arrest. You get the ball rolling Sanjeev, we have him!'

This time Fabio looked him intensely in the eye. Sanjeev averted his gaze, guilty pangs rafting his flanks.

Inspector Sanjeev drove away from Ken Lee Plaza, forcing himself to put Nina out of his mind and concentrate on the immediate job at hand: nailing a murderer. A killer who had entered a beach under cover of darkness and bashed in the skull of a young woman and tossed her away like trash.

Sanjeev's stomach churned when he thought of Valériane and how he had allowed his prejudices to surface above good policing and intuition. He believed that a French woman murdered on the island could only be a crime passionnel.

When Fabio arrived to collaborate, he felt flustered but at the same time inadequate. Could the French authorities have underestimated the capacity of the Mauritian police?

However, as he worked alongside Fabio, he learnt to see things in a different manner. Handling clues with a tacit understanding was key to the two men standing next to each other. One sleek and sly like a fox, the other just ready to enjoy a good meal, sign the register and check out the love of his life. Both men operated differently but were tenacious that the murderer had to be caught as swiftly as possible.

The afternoon dailies printed on the front page 'Valériane Ducasse murderer to be arrested!'.

If it wasn't Inspector Sanjeev's prerogative to alert the journalists of what breaking news was to happen some hundred yards across the corner, it could only come from the tea making corporal who must have overheard or someone eavesdropping from the typing pool next to his office. The walls were of timber ... quite thin!

Either way, news travels very fast on this island. By tomorrow morning, 'the murderer' would have been arrested, judged and sentenced by public opinion. That afternoon, the *dalpuri* seller parked next to the newspaper entrance gate where the papers were sold first, made a good stash. Many regulars on their way home from their respective offices in the capital would grab one newspaper to get the latest news. The mystery killer had given enough fodder to the dailies for months.

Now everyone was eager to know who was the killer.

'Zot pou dire me selma pou tenye en sel kout couma Dantier so ka' said someone who was munching a pair of *dalpuri* while holding his newspaper at an angle to read it.

The *dalpuri* seller had been replying to such questions in his own amiable way.

'*Non, sane foi la, gouvernma français ki lor ka la, pena kata kata la bourzwa*' he said while his hands were in a non-stop movement from one sauce to the other smearing them thinly on the *dalpuris* before folding them in a flash and handed to the customer on a sheet of newsprint paper. This hit home with the Inspector.

Suddenly, without any warning, a downpour hit the warm pedestrian basalt paving filling the

tiny canal alongside it. People huddled against each other. Islanders are notorious when it comes to rain, they avoid it at all cost as if they will melt like sea salt. The *dalpuri* seller made his last roll and closed the lid to his glass carriage holding his empty bowls of *rougay, gros pois curry, achard légumes* and chili paste.

A well-rounded day, he was also ready to head home. Soon, the streets of the city centre would be empty and turn into a ghost town. A new brood would emerge from the under the stones. That of street urchins, drug addicts and prostitutes.

The island was plagued by the drug mafia and substance abusers. As if there was no escape and this was the only way lost souls had to have recourse to end their failures, sorrows and poverty.

Under its purest hues of blues, both of sky and sea, its beguiled idealists and foreign dreamers that it was a peaceful paradise. However, reality choked and shocked those willing to understand beyond this erroneous facade. Mark Twain is long buried and his quote long forgotten.

19

Vadim

Vadim returned from jogging, his vest drenched, his chest heaving and falling as he headed into his apartment. A very faint breeze was circulating, and the cloudless blue sky indicated that this would be another blistering hot day.

He kicked off his sneakers and socks and savoured the coolness that came with bare feet encountering tiles. He pulled off his damp clothes, but did not quite make it to the bathroom before a sparrow demanded entry, hitting the windowpane energetically with his beak.

He was a married man, a rich and busy businessman, flying around the world, who did his own laundry and kept no domestic help at home. His wife never accompanied him on his business trips, such as this one. He had been to and fro when he met Valériane at a bar in a hotel by the coast. The two met a few times until they became lovers. The French scientist showed him something that would act as a magnet between them. They were poles apart and yet spoke one common language. That of pursuing the impossible. Vadim, mostly known as the Russian, became aware through Valériane that the vast Indian Ocean was home to a lost race and civilization. It was not just research but hard facts to support it.

Until one day, Valériane produced diamonds on the side of pebbles on the beach.

The Russian was hooked and latched onto the woman, yet she was elusive as soon as work was at the fore.

Vadim inhaled the fresh salt air and felt a whisper of afternoon breeze against his tanned leathery skin. He opened the window and let in the sparrow who wandered around and promptly flew back out. After refreshing himself, he got to his fishing gear. He threw a length of a mooring line from his boat onto the wooden dock and then jumped off his boat, the Rasputin, his long legs clearing the water between the boat and the dock with ease. The Rasputin, a luxurious runabout for cruising the local waters, was just one of the many yachts he owned. Other days, when he had more time on his hands, he loved to take one of his sailboats out to sea with no destination in mind.

'Yes, sailing boats are the pleasure of my life', Vadim thought to himself. Today's trip, however, was not about pleasure. It had been strictly about business. Landing on the dock with a thud, his well-worn Top-Sider boat shoes worn over his bare feet ensured he didn't slip. He tied the boat up to the dock with a bowline knot, ensuring that the lines were secure.

Cyclone season was coming to an end in the Mauritian sky and ocean, but he wasn't taking any chances with loose moorings.

He tied them short and tight. He paid a crew to always be on hand if needed, although he still liked doing it himself. That way, if something went wrong, he only had himself to blame.

An hour later, he was nearing Château de Mon Plaisir, a colonial mansion sat among acres of sugar cane plantation in the quiet and lush southern part of the island.

He had an important meeting with a sugar baron who had converted himself into one of the richest men in the hospitality industry. Sugar failing, his family had to be quick thinkers and find new ways of making money.

Arriving at the large parking area with centenary trees sprawling their branches loaded with chirping birds, he strode across the rolling lawn towards the large white stucco house hidden from the road by a wrought-iron fence and a colourful hibiscus hedge. The opulent garden was filled with tropical flowers, and the multitude trailing bushes of bougainvillea in fuchsia, peach and white made the place look relaxing. Trees bowed with the weight of ripening mangoes and bananas, and he had to step over several pieces of fruit which had fallen onto the grass. He bent to pick one plump one with its orange reddish belly, but when he turned it up, a coin sized hole looked at him. The bugs or birds were faster than him.

He carried on his way up to the open veranda and out from the shadows came a stout looking woman wearing a crisp white linen apron.

'Bonjour Monsieur'

'Bonjour ! J'ai rendez-vous avec M...' Vadim didn't have time to continue his sentence and he was whisked gently and politely,

without a word, by the lady. She showed him the way to a corridor and then a room. There exuded an air of past luxurious glory in French tones yet all looked tired and outdated, but at least, clean.

'*Monsieur* will be here in a minute, please take a seat. Can I get you any tea, coffee or juice'?

'No, thank you, I am fine.'

He was appreciative that the lady discerned his accent immediately and shifted to a more comfortable English. His French or patois creole had not gotten any better despite his long months of stay on the island.

He was a man of very few words, and socialized to the minimum. In his line of work, this meant class and safety. Two prime elements.

The room was bathed in a cool shade with rectangles of bright light through the colonial chassis of the tall windows. It felt quiet and surprisingly comfortable. Just right for this kind of meeting.

Outside, sprawled a long wrap around veranda. Huge pots of fresh green ferns adorned the empty spaces. It was an airy corner with light metalwork chairs set around tables covered with white linen. The open veranda faced the lush tropical garden where stood majestic royal palm trees, banyan and twisted jasmine vines with bougainvillea bushes. Even the gentle flapping of the rattan screens was regular and soothing.

Suddenly, the silence was interrupted by steps on the bare timber floor. A man appeared. Bespectacled. Medium height, dressed casually in a crumpled white linen shirt and a pair of khaki chino shorts. His tan revealed his long years of being under a tropical sun. He was a local. He lifted his hand as a greeting and Vadim spotted a Nautilus of Philippe Patek watch at his wrist. He wasn't just anybody.

'*Bonjour mon frère*!'

'Bonjour,' Vadim cringed politely. The Russian hated to wait for someone. A good ten minutes were enough to shake his patience but his steely look didn't reveal that change in him.

'So, are we in business my friend? Ready to send truck-loads of the stones?!'

'Yes, we sign and you make the first payment.'

Vadim was in a rush to go. He didn't like the French 'blanc' but he needed him for this new venture. Valériane had left him an incredible possibility of becoming the richest man in Russia within a year. All he needed to do was to remove the precious objects from the sea. As simple as that, in fact, the first harvest amassed a whopping 14 kg of diamonds. Apparently, the whole of the Indian Ocean would house as many creatures living in the depths and reaping them was a colossal fortune.

'*Bien*, looks like Monsieur Boulle is going to bite the dust ...!'

Vadim shook his hand with a brief smile and nodded his way out. He remembered Raymond Boulle, the only billionaire Mauritian to have made a fortune from diamonds. He had read his company's profile on the net.

"*Jean-Raymond Boulle (born 1950) started*

his career at the De Beers Diamond Trading Company ("DTC") where he worked for ten years, in Zaire, Sierra Leone and Antwerp, Belgium. Founder of Diamond Fields

Resources Inc (which Inco purchased for CND$ 4.3 billion), Diamond Fields International Ltd, America Mineral Fields Inc, and Titanium Resources Group Ltd. All four companies are publicly traded companies with deposits of nickel, cobalt, copper, zinc, titanium and diamonds. In 2015, Jean Raymond added a new enterprise to the Jean Boulle Group. Sun King Diamonds Ltd was established to bring an unsurpassed luxurious coating to the yachting, aerospace and automotive world, containing real diamonds. The coating, Sun King Diamond Coating, has since then graced supercars, a Global Bombardier private jet, superyachts and *several sublime pieces of art."*

Outside, the air felt refreshing. Vadim bid goodbye to the French man and saw a discreet head peeking from behind the curtain. It was the woman who showed him in. The islanders are good information archivists, they have their ways to gather intel. He was glad he didn't keep such housekeeping helpers. Privacy was key to him. He drove out of the estate and couldn't help admiring the huge fanned traveller's palms. The line of royal palms standing majestic against the sky, just oozing that air of a tropical haven.

The day was good. He continued his way to the north of the island, feeling the need to switch on the a/c as he moved past the high plateau to the descent onto the coastal plains. He had a mission now, and it had started the night Valériane died. She wanted

$500,000 for some diamonds and disclosing an absurd secret. All she wanted was funding for her lab facing cuts from a mafia of scientists wanting her project. Vadim trusted and gave her the money. In return, she led him to the way of becoming richer than Crésus.

Life was awful for many on this island, but a boon for some like treasure seekers like Vadim.

The Devil doesn't knock twice at one's door, went the adage ...

20

Sirens

They say you can sail a thousand miles along the island chain of the Mû, from the sandy shores of the north, to the lush, sultry islands of the south.

They say that the islanders are like the red crabs that race along the shores – hardy, unpredictable, and as happy in the water as out of it.

They say that the ocean around the Mû has its own madness. Sailors tell of great whirlpools that swallow boats, and of reeking, fierce water jets that bubble to the surface and stop the hearts of swimmers. Black clouds suddenly boil into existence amid flawless blue skies.

They say that there is a dark realm of nightmares that lie beneath the true sea. When the undersea arches its back, the upper sea is stirred into frenzy.

They say that the undersea was the dwelling place of the gods.

They say many things about Mû, and all of them are true.

The gods were as real as the coastlines and currents, and as merciless as the winds and whirlpools. For centuries the gods ruled Mû through awe and terror, each with its own cluster of islands as territory. Human sacrifices were hurled into the waters to appease them, and every boat was painted with pleading eyes to entreat their mercy. They were served, feared and adored.

Then, without warning, the gods turned on each other. It took barely a week for them to tear one another apart – a week of tidal waves and devastation.

Many hundreds of islanders lost their lives. By the end, no living gods remained, only vast corpses rolling into the deep. Even thirty thousand years after this, nobody knows why it happened. The gods are still mysterious, though the fear of them is slowly waning. They say that a coin-sized scrap of dead god can make your fortune, if the powers it possesses are strange and rare enough, and if you are brave enough to dive for them.

This is also true.

Down the docks of the old harbour the large old building was deliberately misshapen, its roofline bulging and deformed, its windows ragged crevices like rips in the stonework. The marine air and water had dug circular grooves in the stones making fossil-like patterns of ammonites.

Even so long after the death of the gods, everyone still knew that the sacred were twisted.

There was a beauty that belonged only to the gods, and it was a knot in your eye, your gut, your mind . . . When a governor general of an island had taken over the island, by the simple, honest method of having lots of armed men and declaring that he'd done so, he'd been too canny to take the great building at the top of the steps for his residence. Instead, he'd had a clean, white house of brick built not far from the docks, with a protective surrounding wall. He'd understood that the old priests' hall was a link to a sick past. It was beneath him.

Therefore, he'd had it converted into an auction house. There were petty auctions every week, selling off salvage, ordinary cargoes and confiscated goods.

A *vente à l'encan* was a grand auction, a chance to buy ships, the finest luxuries from pirates. Nowadays, the only thing they could boast more of than other islands was crime. Nobody knew that the building used to be a temple and was older than the surfaced island's shores.

In theory, slavery was forbidden within the Mû. However, if you were judged guilty of a crime, you could be sold as an 'indentured servant'.

All the islands of the Mû respected the indentures. If they did not, how could they buy criminals for the jobs nobody wanted? The worse your crime, the longer the time you had to serve. If you tried to run away, you could be caught and dragged back to your 'owner', who might punish you or sell you to someone worse. There was always someone worse.

The great hall was designed to make people feel like ants. You knew it as soon as you walked in. It was too open, too vast, its vaulted ceiling too high, the windows too narrow and lofty, the shafts of light from them too dim. Even the two dozen rows of benches put out for auction buyers filled only half the hall. Human crowds were lost in it. Voices rebounded oddly, the echoes sounding higher and more startled than the original voice.

Jonas was deep in his lecture. The venue chosen was odd but he didn't mind the humidity of the air.

An old barge building by the harbour, couldn't have been more apt for the theme of today's talk. 'The world of sirens' He had fun relating to his audience a subject which wasn't often talked about.

« *The siren cycle plays out something like this: When the time is right, usually shortly after puberty, she will leave the ocean in search of a mate.*

The urge to procreate becomes more powerful than the desire to stay in the ocean, so she leaves her watery home until she falls in love, and eventually produces a child. She adopts a human form and lifestyle in order to do so. Like many sea-dwelling creatures, sirens have long lifespans. They are picky about their mates so even if it takes years to find one, they'll stay on land until it happens.

Once on land, sirens are able to flush themselves with fresh water to suppress the instinct that is enhanced by salt in order to stay on land as long as is needed. They can swim in salt water during this phase as long as they keep themselves hydrated with fresh water.

In a way, the fresh water makes them forget their siren selves. At the moment, some of them feel almost fully human and barely feel the need to swim at all.

When a siren falls in love, she fully intends to stay with her mate forever and live the rest of her life on land. If the man is old fashioned, as my father was, they marry.

To a siren, the idea of marriage is foreign. After all, she's a sea creature and not attached to human customs, but she usually goes along with the ceremony to make her lover happy.

Soon, she becomes pregnant and goes through all of the same nesting phases that a human woman would. But after the birth of a child, things slowly begin to change. If the child is a daughter, her mother will take her to the ocean under cover of darkness. The exposure to seawater triggers the siren gene and the girl's legs morph into their true form, a powerful tail.

 In a sense, it is a second birth. When sirens talk about their birth, they always mean their salt-birth – the moment they first took *their siren shape. Mother and daughter might live on land with this secret for a while to allow the child to grow sufficiently strong to survive in the ocean.*

Even then, the siren will have lapses where she desires to stay on land with her family. This transition phase is very difficult emotionally. The siren bond to her mate is strong, but the call of the ocean will always win in the end.

The father would never know what really happened, and if she's done a good job keeping her identity secret, he would never know that he had married a siren. In cases where the siren leaves without preparing for it, there is a missing person's report and a protracted search, which always fails. She'll have vanished without a trace. »

Jonas switched off the projector and readied

himself for questions from the audience. He noticed regulars to his talks, Fabio the French detective alongside Inspector Sanjeev.

They both didn't leave him from their sights. Jonas felt uneasy and made a sign to the audience that he shall take a short break. He left the podium and went behind the room separators. He had only just sat down and was ready to drink some water when both the detective and the inspector appeared in front of him.

'Hello Professor Jonas, all good?'

'Y ...yes indeed! Glad to see you in the audience. Do sirens interest you both so much?'

'Maybe you can tell us more about them at the police station' answered Inspector

Sanjeev promptly, far too ready and impatient for the next action.

'Professor Jonas you are under arrest related to the murder of Professor Valériane Ducasse' in a metallic click, a pair of handcuffs caught

Jonas wrists without him realizing what was happening.

'But you are mad! You have no right! Me a murderer?! Is this a joke? Fabio ... What about my audience? They are expecting me. This is ridiculous.'

Fabio presented the arrest warrant which silenced Jonas and he followed the two men reluctantly. Outside, the audience was quite raucous, so no one had witnessed that the professor had been whisked away. They would have to hold back their questions.

Inspector Sanjeev made his appearance at Ah Cheew's eatery harbouring a wide smile. Nina was happy to see him, he had made himself rare these days he had been hanging out with the French detective. Ah Cheew replied to his cheerful greeting with a fake smile. She had read about the arrest in the afternoon paper and it was splashed on the front pages the next morning.

'What an ungrateful man! All that good food I fed him and he didn't even pipe me a word...pfff!'

Ah Cheew couldn't mask her discontentment vis a vis the inspector. According to her, he should have hushed her to the secret of the arrest. If only he knew how many long sleepless nights this whole investigation had given her! And Nina. Oh, that's another sad story.

Ah Cheew thought better not look in the direction of the young cook. Her day might be spoiled for good. She was tempted to sack her but for … what?! Nina had not wronged her at all professionally.

To that thought, she gulped in a rice mochi, a latest addition to her confectionary collection she sold as a mouth sweetener after a hot spicy meal. The sweet sticky dough managed to calm her brain. She learnt the Japanese recipe on YouTube.

She glanced in the inspector's direction, he was enjoying a bowl of shrimp wonton soup - on the day's menu, dowsing it with red homemade *mazavaroo*.

'Ah!' Sighed Ah Cheew.

After having fed himself well, Inspector

Sanjeev went back to his office. He felt excited like a boy in front of a new toy. It wasn't every day that such arrests happen. Fabio sat in the next room, looked at the sheets of paper in front of him and began to taste being puzzled for the first time in his career.

Never before had he had such little inclination about a suspect. Sure, he'd been wrong in the past, way off the mark even, but at least that set off a chain of thought that led to him being right. Right now, the picture he could paint was abstract, and he absolutely hated abstract paintings.

He had a dislike for anything that wasn't practical – this island included.

He longed for the claustrophobic streets of Paris where he got his training from, where the buildings stopped nature from making his eyes itch and his nose burn.

Most of all, he despised and feared the people here. Never had he seen such collective arrogance and entitlement. Every question and answer given to him in each interview screamed self-service.

The pressure was on to get a result before people started arguing their rights to leave the island. The truth was that any of them could leave if they wanted to, but they knew that the finger of guilt would point right at them. He had only one interview to conduct, and although he held little hope for an admission, he was particularly interested in the outcome.

For it didn't stop there.

He reached Inspector Sanjeev's office in three leg lengths and asked him to get ready for more arrests.

'What are you saying? I thought we had arrested the culprit.' Sanjeev let out a burp in between looking genuinely surprised. Fabio sometimes wondered whether the policeman had really been trained. His incredulity was baffling.

'Non...non, this was only a bait, and a part of a gang. Others are out there, we haven't caught the head yet. He would be vigilant. Now, stop all boats from leaving the shore for longer hauls. Nobody should leave the island without official permission. Alert the National Coast Guard and the helicopter squad.'

'Alright, it will be done asap! ... waiting and expecting to be debriefed as soon as you can.'

Fabio turned his back and went outside for a fag. Inspector Sanjeev watched him while slumped at the desk, frustration coming out of his pores. It was like watching a vegan trying to work out the best way to carve a chicken. Why couldn't he have the results that the Frenchie had? He always thought of Professor Jonas as an intelligent idiot who couldn't string a sentence together without giving lengthy explanations.

But now though, he saw a man in too deep. He seemed powerless, defeated, resigned to the powers that be. Who were those powers? There were some things that he had helped kill. Slip of the tongue? Unfortunate coincidence? Sanjeev tried hard to convince himself of either, but in the end, he settled on it being more sinister. No, Jonas' story wasn't just to fill a gap in the papers. It wasn't part of the narrative, or a public service. It was calculated. It was an exercise in deflection, ordered by a killer.

The matter was serious. In his heart, he couldn't stop admiring Fabio. That man had something in him. He had the flair that justified his reputation.

*

Inspector Sanjeev was fuming. One of the main tabloids had splashed its first page in the style they always do. Judgment by journalistic fodder, and shamelessly so. Inducing the public in error while getting high TRPs.

"Investigating officers refused to contribute to our story, citing the ongoing investigation and respect for the deceased as a reason to keep certain details private. Thoughts from the guests on the island, however, take a different view of why they refused to comment.

"It's embarrassing for the police to have no solid suspects after 24 hours. Meanwhile, late Prof Ducasse's husband is heartbroken, her colleagues are in mourning and we're stuck here with a cold-blooded killer. It would seem that much will happen over the next 24 hours, and there is a sincere hope on MURDER ISLAND that the killer will be identified and arrested. In the meantime, the guests look set to stay put, with the great fear of seeming guilty by leaving. Most are quietly keeping to themselves and updating their families on their wellbeing. Others, however, are already despicably capitalizing on Mrs Valériane Ducasse's murder – using it to grow followers or deflect from other DISGRACEFUL scandals they may be involved in. The sad fact that some would seek to gain from such a tragedy paints a very stark picture of celebrity culture and our society in general …

"For live, uninterrupted, 24/7 coverage and updates on the investigation, visit our blog."

The Police Press office had sent a release to the dailies about the arrest.

Why has it been reported that no suspects have been arrested?

Inspector Sanjeev smelled a conspiracy at the brim. This affair was far deeper than he thought. There were some bigwigs involved surely, otherwise who could influence the island's biggest and most respected daily to publish such an intentional omission.

Ah Cheew was in a better mood and kept on her transistor by her side playing some Chinese songs. They made no sense to her as she didn't understand Mandarin apart from a few words here and there. But listening to the Asian songs kept her grounded.

She was of the generation who was born much after her great grandfathers came to the island as merchants.

The British allowed many Chinese to the island to try their luck at what others before them were muddled up in understanding. Trapped in either an abolished state of slavery but well attached to their plantations, many African descents straddled upon the indentured labourers for a clash of identity.

But how on earth were there so many Indians on the island? Freedom is not bought and certainly not distributed freely. Unlike in SE Asian countries where they were regularly prey to wild animals and eaten from plantations. Probably even more from the native-owned estates but there are no records there. The simplest explanation was that labour was a cheap commodity, therefore the labourers' lives are cheap and one man taken is one-man fewer to feed, house and pay... and there will be plenty more waiting to take his place.

Somehow, the Chinese chose to stay within the city centre as compared to the Indians who lived scattered in the countryside tending to their lands. The Chinese were here to make quick money, not wasting time. And the city centre was just right for that with the appropriate crowd.

Ah Cheew enjoys the quietness of the streets during Sundays when all the shops are closed. Talk, laughter, mock-quarrels and the clatter of mah-jong tiles floated through the open windows at all hours. She could guess what went on inside the homes. Food and congregating around the dinner table. Long lunches followed by mah-jong games ending the late afternoons before preparing stocks for the next morning. The Chinese folk were always busy. They would stop working only once a year. That's for the New Year. Ah Cheew followed the tradition and she believed in financial success out of this life of sacrifice.

The Chinese way is to keep quiet and try to stay unnoticed and out of trouble. It doesn't always work. At least Ah Cheew wasn't of that breed. Her life's passion revolved around her kitchen and her interest around people's lives. She loved being in 'the know'. How Inspector Sanjeev left her out of the news of the arrest of the suspect in the murder of the 'beach body' has put a dent in her views and affection for the policeman. It was sheer betrayal. She spent the night ruminating over the whys and it only ended up giving her a headache. But true to herself, she tamed her irritability over the matter and decided to address it in the true style of Ah Cheew - Confront Inspector Sanjeev. She could still see him how he was enjoying his meal yesterday while sending smiles to Nina.

Well, that romance could be short lived. And he would expect to be left high and dry just when he was shaping his future move with the young cook.

'Li pou conné are moi ! Capave croire ...' muttered Ah Cheew with a nervous quiver on her chin.

She likes to be 'informed' of what's going on in people's lives around her and all gossip she calls news. Anything that disrupts her endeavours to get some 'news' does not go down well.

Even summoning of Buddha would not change the rattiness which had taken over Ah Cheew.

21

Freedom

Beautiful, she was.

Despite her thinness, Mûra had an exotic, almost unnatural, beauty.

Her skin appeared dark most of the time, in a tropical islander's way, but when light from the window passed over her as the sun broke through, she somehow appeared much paler. Her grey brown eyes changed the way fast-moving clouds did on a stormy day, sometimes there was a flash of blue, other times a flash of green. She had small pointed ears, one of which stood out starkly against her hair as she'd tucked her long locks behind them. And her cheekbones were high enough to make her appear elven. Her hair seemed like a being all on its own. From closer, one could see that it was lighter and puffier than any hair, each strand so fine that the lightest breeze could lift it and make it sway. It looked like spider's silk without the stickiness.

It now floated over her shoulders like a thick cloud, spilling across the pillow and bedsheets on either side of her hips. Her bodice of her robe was encrusted with aquamarines and large diamonds, glittering as she turned this way and that. Kohl look alike lined her eyes and coloured powders accented her cheekbones and lips and gave an iridescent glow each time they caught light.

It reminded Fabio of the mermaid and unicorn merchandise little girls play with and surround themselves with.

He suddenly felt guilty to always have disregarded these details as childish and tacky. In fact, it is through the eyes of children that truth reveals itself. Their innocence allows their worlds to be plumped by many wonderful details adults cannot perceive. Their imaginary world is simply ... beyond imaginary. It was the lucidity of innocence.

A light breeze blew in through the window. The smell of the ocean was healing her faster than any food or drink ever could.

"Breaking a curse is not a simple matter," she uttered mentally sending the message to the white man in front of her.

"A curse takes on the nature of the being who created it, and curses are rarely made by those with kind hearts. If you want to know more about this, you should prepare yourself. There's more to what the eyes can see" Mûra continued the telepathic exchange to Fabio who was totally enthralled by this sea being. He had all his doubts and assurance that whatever he searched for was unbelievable but having this creature in front of him ... unsettled his understanding. He wanted to turn into the little boy he was in his childhood reading about the Little Mermaid and the universe of fantastic beings that fascinated him. But this ...this was real!

Mûra spoke to the man as she felt his heart was kind with a genuine force for justice. She was ready to reveal about her species and how they have been trapped and preyed upon.

Fabio pieced the huge underlying mystery with a fervour that laid unmatched in all his career. It came in disjointed bits of information, because whoever took the photographs wasn't concerned about the story of the curse so much as the nature of the gemstones. Pure greed of men. Total disregard for human life or nature. His assessment of Prof Jonas was priceless as he found himself in his trust sharing more than should have been done, was it by arrogance of knowing far more than the layman? Or the stupidity that criminals make?

Whatever it was, Prof Jonas eventually cracked after two days of interrogation and revealed the network to him. And through him, he was able to reach to deliver this poor sea creature held captive in a mini pool under a hangar. He was stunned by her beauty but the raw scars on her body showed how mercilessly she had been robbed of the gems that constitute her skin. Her aggressors could only have been the vilest of creatures - men! They exist even in this land called paradise. They are everywhere. Their reach is further than where the eyes meet the horizon line.

These sea creatures have been hiding in the depths for eons out of the wrath of a great priestess who was betrayed, but innocents pay for the mistakes of those in power. They reap despair and tumult without a node of hope or redemption.

Fabio in his Gaelic mindset was beginning to understand what a curse was, and it was unbearable even to a human mind. No wonder curses were often relegated to hell. A curse is evil. Surely nature was not pleased with it. Sirens certainly were not, but this curse was so old that most didn't even know it was a curse anymore. Fabio had to re-concentrate to continue talking to Mûra. He had heard of telepathic exchanges and it was easier than he thought it was, simply focus and the conversation starts. Tacitly, in all silence.

'Can you tell me where you come from and how it is?'

'The continent of Mû sprawls around the whole of the Indian Ocean. It was a sprawling but organized metropolis, with a main port to the ocean and an outer and inner ring of riverways. These passageways for deliveries in and out of Mû were wide and deep. With many ports along its waterfront, it was easy to distribute goods and travellers to anywhere in Mû.

The very centre of it was reserved for wealthy residences, glittering temples, and rich gardens fed with freshwater diverted from the high waterfalls to the north. Fresh spring water both hot, from the thermals, and cold, from deeper underground, was fed through pipelines to every home. Everyone, no matter how young or old, how rich or poor, had access to fresh water. Every family was given a small plot of land for a garden.

Sometimes only a few square meters of soil, but it was enough to feed four if well-tended. At the heart of Mû was an exquisite temple with fat white pillars and a huge dome with an oculus. This way nothing would be hidden from the gods and all activities would be lit with either sunlight or moonlight.

Directly beneath the oculus was a pool fed directly from the ocean itself. Saltwater, though a deity for the Mer, was also revered by Mûrians, for the ocean is what gave the nation its power.'

Mûra looked paler from the strain of 'talking' to Fabio and the detective waved a hand asking her to rest. He went outside and lit a cigarette as a break for himself.

All this was invraisemblable ... how could he write his report with such details? After discovering about the horrors of the diamonds and aquamarines of the sea creatures, Fabio felt a gut repulsion for the gems. The stories of the blood diamonds in Africa were not the only aggressive assaults men did to fellow men, but their grip also transcended to unknown worlds. This was even worse.

Fabio remembered one of his missions in Namibia which taught him a lesson of humility. He had also met colleagues in Sierra Leone on the braconnage of blood diamonds.

It is tempting to view diamonds as a fixed part of life. In our time they represent a ubiquitous luxury, an incessantly advertised object, and, to many, a classic symbol of love and wealth.

Owners of a diamond have a sense that it emerges in stages: by nature, by a miner's labour, and then by a cutter's skill. Less appreciated is how a diamond is an invented product. Outside of limited and relatively recent industrial uses, a diamond's consumption historically has much more to do with prestige than with utility. Arguably no place on earth better illustrates that principle than does Namibia, formerly the colony known as German Southwest Africa.

For hundreds of years, Namibia's Indigenous people had little use for diamonds, regarding them as objects to which they attached no value and which they generally let sit in the sand.

Outsiders often proved similarly indifferent. In the late nineteenth century, when Europeans combed the Namib Desert hoping to find a diamond consistent with the image of jewellery glamorized in the West, they ignored millions of rough diamonds that, in an unaltered state, resembled shards of glass and thus carried no social weight.

The sky had taken a peaceful light sapphire wash with puffs of darker grey in the distance. Surely rain was coming fast. Fabio enjoyed his last puff before squashing the butt and taking in a breath of fresh air before going inside. He had to learn more from

Mûra. The siren looked better and her eyes glittered with more life. She gave him a slight bow. Fabio was taken aback

 by this stance. It was so unexpected. He shook his head in acknowledgement. He learnt this response from his missions in the Far East. It meant 'am with you'.

Fabio started his conversation 'I see you are feeling better, I am glad.'

'Thank you, yes I feel your positive energy. You are a good spirit.' The spirit part gave Fabio an uneasiness.

In the mortal world only, the deceased were called spirits, but in the fantastical world and beyond it probably had its own real meaning. Spirits are eternal entities attached to living beings.

'What I find strange is how you were caught

and robbed of your gems? Did you trust humans to go close to them?'

'Yes and no. We have lived among them watching them for far too long. My sisters and I found a kind blonde lady who used to watch us every night, and she would stay for long on the beach, quietly. We got used to her and accepted her presence just like any other creature. Once, she even helped one of us to the water when she got too dehydrated staying far too long in the woods.'

'So, what happened? Did she attack you after that?'

'No ... she brought a man. A tall big man. His spirit was dark. We had recognised him from his hatch in the sea, he often passed with huge speed hurting our cousins the dolphins who got too close. He would also catch marlins and other swordfish who battled for their life in a long trail of blood. My sisters tried to help deliver them but alas their hooks in their guts were too strong. We watched them die helplessly.'

*

Tall big man in a yacht? Fabio's mind raced to one such man with his detective's mind; Vadim the Russian! He had been on his radar although he never spoke about him to Inspector Sanjeev. Fearing the evil spider of influence on the rampage on the island corrupting all those willing.

'So?'

'The golden hair lady came with him one night, and what we saw made us cry salty tears, but it was too late, he had already seen us.'

'Why did you cry?'

'Owww ...' Mûra lets out a gentle howl on a trans piercing high pitch. Fabio had to close his ears.

'Stop!' The siren obeyed. Fabio opened his eyes and looked deeply in the flooded ones of the sea creatures which were shining with gold.

'What happened?'

'The big tall man ... he hit the golden hair lady with a stone, she fell and didn't get up again. We kept on waiting to see her getting up. She didn't. He then took her on a boat and dropped her in the sea. We tried reviving her, but she was gone. So, we helped drift her towards the shore.'

Fabio slammed his fist against the wall, and winced in pain. 'I knew it!'

All went quiet. The siren closed her eyes in

what seemed a sob. She turned her back to Fabio. The detective had nothing else to ask her for now. She had just helped him crack the case in the most unbelievable way. How he can present this evidence was the now biggest challenge for him.

*

Arresting Vadim was easy. The Russian was in his den and provided no resistance to him being handcuffed. However, his sly smile came when he started being interrogated.

'Do you even know why you arrested me? How can you prove that I stole gems from sirens?!...who will believe this insane story? Wait until you hear from my lawyers, you have no idea with whom you are toying with now!'

'No, Mr Vadim, we have arrested you for the

murder of Prof Valériane Ducasse, as for the gems you will tell us the story yourself.'

'I need my lawyers!'

'Rest assured, you will get everything, but for now there's a very slim sliver of hope to save you from the heinous crimes you committed. Get used to the food here, it will be good for you.'

Fabio left the interrogation chamber and met with other officers and Inspector Sanjeev outside. The latter's grimacing face had still not lost the countenance of an octopus changing their hues. He certainly felt at a loss with such a monumental unfolding of the case. As an islander, he couldn't even have guessed that such a denouement could exist. Inside, as a Mauritian, he felt jubilantly proud thinking that after all 'we are not that poor as a nation, there's royalty in our blood, that of a mighty race - the Mûrians.'

However, facing Fabio made him feel diminished and felt he could recoil in his shell. Losing face was an understatement, he doubted the reason for his wearing his police uniform.

Could people see through his frailty and lack of sharpness of mind? One murder happened that shook the city folks and he couldn't even understand the whys and wherefores. He felt like going to Nina and hiding his face on her shoulder. He shuddered at the thought.

Ah Cheew towered over him like a Chinese green dragon with fiery eyes ready to gulp him alive. Life wasn't fair. He couldn't go out, couldn't stay in the office, then where to hide his face and seek solace?

He looked ahead at the tall window and saw the *poudine maïs* seller on his bicycle. Yes, that was one guy who always treated him well.

'*Bonzour Bourzwa, ki li dire*?' He would say each time and give him a large slice of sweet *poudine maïs* covered with fresh grated coconut. He just needed that break now, and with someone who could respect him. He needed to feel it in all his pores. He took his *képi* and headed to the *marsan poudine*.

Fabio was grilling a cigarette outside and greeted him.

'Lunch later? Same place?'

Inspector Sanjeev, hesitated, stammered and eventually gave a positive nod. He couldn't say no to Fabio. The guy has earned enough respect from him to enthral his mind as to how he cracked this murder mystery that even the colline citadel couldn't shake.

He thought maybe seeing Nina would be good. Her presence could be a balm to his battered ego and self-confidence right now. He gave a nod to Fabio.

The loud horns on the street brought him to reality, the *marsan* had already spotted him and was smiling with his two and half tooth pegs showing menacingly in their greyish brown hues. Looks like the leftover *poudine maïs* had a sure regular taker. The tooth rot spilled the beans.

After a copious meal of Thursday specials, both Fabio and Inspector Sanjeev opted for a cool chocolate and vanilla ice cream. A treat but also to cool down the hot spicy sauce they both dunked in their dumplings copiously. Chayote and river shrimps steamed Niouk Yen dumplings were hard to resist.

Nina brought them an extra plate each while Ah Cheew got up from her vigil point. She was beaming to see Sanjeev after so long, and the latter was blushing like a young cockerel.

Ah Cheew came back and gave them a long stare. Heavy with resentment. But for today, both men were feeling light and didn't bother about her mood.

When they left, Ah Cheew pointed her finger to Inspector Sanjeev, the latter turned away his face pretending he was invisible.

'So, what do we do with the siren?'

'Look after her, we still have to ask her some questions. And get a forensic person to get support as to how intel gathered by telepathy can be a proof of evidence in the case of murder. She and her species have to be protected and we have to make sure that not a word goes out to the outer world.'

'Then, we embrace the murder case, right?!'

'Yes, indeed, that's all we have got. It will be a hard report to write and submit to the court.'

'We shall do it … we can do it.'

Fabio knew that he could trust Sanjeev over this, he had his heart in the right place. Besides, he would have his whole life to thread the stories of sirens to his future kids. Pirates have always been more popular as sea stories in Mauritius, but sirens … no. The islanders don't even know that not far from them, lived Manatees in the Mozambican channel.

*

Mûra recuperated fast under the care of Fabio who made sure she was surrounded by trustworthy people to look after her round the clock. He visited her daily.

Some days, just sitting quietly and enjoying the company of each other. On one such day, she began to sing, a siren tone that had a multi-layered, musical quality, like harmonizing violins. It was exquisitely beautiful, sounds like it was coming from everywhere, and was completely irresistible to the human ear.

Fabio heard it for the first time and remembered the account of Jonas' own experience, who almost got himself drowned had he not been called by a stranger on the beach.

Fabio knew Mûra was ready to join her brood out in freedom. Somewhere, somehow, he had got used to the presence of the siren. It soothed and mesmerized him. He felt selfish but then shook the thought, for the time he spent there was vital to gather as much information so as to protect her species for a long time. With all his knowledge of the destructive power men had, he couldn't allow them to be rediscovered by such greedy beings. He felt ashamed to be part of such a lowly species called humans.

All the academic flow about the evolution of men was in fact a regressive mode where morals and ethics were concerned. And greed! Just for 'paper' money. From hunter gatherers dressed in animal hide, men had evolved into the most ruthless predator the earth had produced. Far mightier than the dinosaurs whose small brains didn't hatch perpetual evil plans to do harm to one another, out of sheer lowly intentions. Not for finding food for survival like in the animal kingdom.

Men were armed with killer brains and extended their knowledge into making killer arms with the sheer intention to destroy and kill. Fabio walked to Mûra, stood in front of her and mentally asked her silently 'so are you ready to go?'

Mûra looked at him, gave him the most beautiful iridescent blink of her eye and replied 'I have always been ready to be freed. I need my elemental water to exist. You have been good to me and I am grateful for that, should you ever need me, just call ... I will come.'

Fabio lowered his eyes, he couldn't believe that parting ways with the siren would be so hard to his heart. It wasn't love, it wasn't lust, it wasn't friendship but a visceral bond that he couldn't understand. Probably it accounts from the origins of Man which started in the oceans. Some stayed there and evolved half fish half human bearing an evolutionary advancement over other faculties that men lost when they touched land.

Mûra continued singing and there was an air of joy in the tone. Fabio felt peaceful and content. That's one murder case that will leave his heart and mind marked forever. His rational thinking has made a dent for the good side. He promised to read and document himself more about our species and those men related to fantasy.

For truth often hides what's essential to the

eye. Fabio looked again at Mûra and told her imploringly with great sadness how sorry he was for all the harm she and her sisters had suffered at the hands of men. He vowed that she will be protected from now onwards. In the deep silence of his conscience, he could hear the moans of the wounded and the dying filling the narrow valley.

The full moon, big and bright and already high in the sky, cast its cold blue light over the washed deserted beach. All looked peaceful.

Life continues, on land, in air, deep down in the sea.

Tales will be told. Mûra joined her element in freedom and peace ... for now.